I Came
to the Highlands

Also by Velda Johnston

THE WHITE PAVILION
MASQUERADE IN VENICE
THE LATE MRS. FONSELL
THE MOURNING TREES
THE FACE IN THE SHADOWS
THE PEOPLE ON THE HILL
THE LIGHT IN THE SWAMP
THE PHANTOM COTTAGE
I CAME TO A CASTLE
A HOWLING IN THE WOODS
HOUSE ABOVE HOLLYWOOD
ALONG A DARK PATH

I Came
to the Highlands

A NOVEL OF SUSPENSE

by Velda Johnston

Dodd, Mead & Company * New York

ISBN: 0-396-06950-9
Library of Congress Catalog Card Number: 74-96
Printed in the United States of America
by Vail-Ballou Press, Inc., Binghamton, N.Y.

For Joe and Mimi Hammond, who know why

I Came
to the Highlands

One

It is late July now. This morning, after sprinkling dried lavender among the newly woven sheets in the upstairs linen press, I went to the window of my husband's room and mine and looked out.

Our twin daughters were not in sight, but I could hear them from beyond the big lilac bush in the dooryard, squabbling mildly over whose turn it was to rock the doll cradle their father built for their sixth birthday last March. In the hay field across the road my husband and my fourteen-year-old son—my son, but not my husband's—reaped the long grass, their scythes flashing in the sunlight. Above their heads, meadowlarks circled on stubby triangular wings.

As I stood there, I experienced that sense of timelessness which, I suppose, comes to all of us now and then. Always, I felt, summer would be at its full. Always my daughters would rock their cradle beside a lilac bush which would never lose its leaves. And those same larks, spilling song from their throats, would circle always above my husband's rough dark head and Will's fiery red one.

Such moments are good. But there are moments when my sense of time plays less pleasant tricks, moments when the barrier of years seems to crumble, and the tumultuous past rushes in on the peaceful present, like the storm-driven tides which sometimes break through the dunes to flood our Long Island meadows with salt. Such a moment came one day last September, when Will and I were harvesting beach plums near Shinnecock Bay. Hands busy among the stiff-leaved bushes, I looked up to see that my son, a pail still in his hand, had climbed a dune to gaze out over the water. At that moment his resemblance was so strong to that other red-haired young man—standing with bare legs knee-deep in bracken in that wild northern country across the sea—that I felt suddenly faint. The serene September sky seemed to darken. Once more I seemed to stand, penniless and bewildered, on the stones of that castle courtyard, with my father's sagging weight heavy against my shoulder, and a woman I had never seen before staring at me with unmistakable hatred through the murky red glow of the torches. Once more I felt the bog in Bowain Wood drag at my floundering body, and heard, with mingled hope and dread, the pound of approaching feet. And once again, in the icy starlight, I clung with half-frozen hands to the side of the round tower, aware that on the parapet above someone waited—waited for my numb fingers to lose their grip and let me plunge with my unborn child to shatter on the rocks below.

Will turned. Like the child he so recently was, he allowed his feet almost to slide out from under him as he descended the dune. The memory of a desperate night in a far country receded. Once again it was a sunny September afternoon in the year of our Lord, 1765. Once again I was no longer young and terrified and alone, but a respected housewife in His Majesty's Colony of Southampton, surrounded by neighbors who do not know of my son's origin, and who seem to have forgiven, if not forgotten, that engaging rascal, my father, whom they once banished from their midst.

Not that he ever seemed a rascal to me. Nor was it just because I was motherless from the age of thirteen that I loved him so. Even before that summer when deadly fever swept Southampton, and my father and I walked hand in hand behind the coffin to one of the new graves in the burial ground at the foot of our street, Job's Lane, I had adored him. And he had charm for other females besides myself. As I passed from childhood to young girlhood, I became increasingly aware that even the most sedate of the village matrons became brighter of eye and cheek whenever, on the elm-shaded streets, Schoolmaster Walter Logan bowed to her.

True, he had a great weakness. He drank. Many a night in our little house I was awakened by the sound of his stumbling progress along the lower hall and up the stairs to his room opposite mine. But I knew that in the morning, sober if not always steady-handed, he would be at his desk in the parlor, facing the farmers' and merchants' sons into whose sometimes thick heads he strived to instill reading, arithmetic, and at least a smattering of Latin and Greek. What was more, I knew that many other men, including some of the most prominent in our village, repaired nightly to the tavern. Tosspots themselves, they could scarcely complain that Walter Logan set a bad example for their sons.

No, I am sure that what irritated Southampton men

3

was my father's elegance of speech, dress, and manner, an elegance which brought that arch look to their wives' faces and which, here in this village where everyone worked, seemed a galling reminder of that class-ridden country which they or their ancestors had fled. More than once I had to fight down rage when I heard some grown person refer to Walter Logan's "airs." And once, in the lower hall of our house, I slapped the face of a boy who had just said to his snickering classmates, in an accent that imitated my father's, "Gad, sirs, but you are a pack of numbskulls."

Passionately I felt that my father had a right to his polished manners, and to the glossy brown peruke that covered his graying hair, and to the smart breeches and coats that set off his trim figure—not homespun coats and breeches, such as other Southampton men wore, but clothing tailored for him in Boston. Was he not, after all, the nephew of a Scottish baronet, Sir James Macduveen of Bowain Castle?

Even when I was a little girl, he talked to me freely about that castle in the Scottish Highlands, and those relatives I had never seen. He told me that my great-uncle James, the baronet, was a stern man who, unlike many Scots, was a staunch supporter of the Church of England and of those plump Hanoverian monarchs who had replaced the handsome and graceful Stuarts on the British throne. He told me of James Macduveen's beautiful and tragic young sister, my great-aunt Arabella, who only months after her marriage, and for reasons unknown, had drowned herself in a deep loch a few miles from Bowain Castle. Of his father—my grandfather, Malcolm Macduveen—he could tell me little at first hand. A mettlesome horse had thrown Malcolm, breaking his neck, a few months before my father was born. "But I fear," my father would say with a mock-rueful smile, "that he was a bit of a scapegrace, fond of his port and his malt, and with a quick eye for a pretty face."

Again and again, at my urging, he would take down the geography from which he taught his pupils, and show me the map of Scotland. "Here is the tiny village of Garlaig," he would say, "and here is where Bowain Castle stands, its rear windows looking across the strait at the Island of Skye." As he talked, I felt I could almost see the shimmering strait and, beyond it, the cloud-wreathed mountains of Skye. I felt I could see the castle with its two round towers and its high-walled courtyard. "It is not a large castle, Bess, and not old, as age is considered in such matters. The first baronet built it in the fifteen-hundreds. And of course it has been many generations since the Macduveens had to use it to defend their lands."

Almost everywhere, he told me, the Highlands are haunted by the sound of moving water—the slow, deep rhythms of breakers on ocean beaches, the quicker lapping of wavelets on the shores of inland lochs, and the murmurs of burns rushing down mountainsides, dark brown except where boulders break them into foamy white. And sometimes, to make me laugh, he would drop into the dialect of uneducated Scotsmen, his speech filled with sounds made far back in his throat, and studded with strange words—"shieling" for meadow, and "bairn" for child, and "ill-shaken-up" for awkward.

But fond as he was of such talk, there were some aspects of his early years he would discuss only reluctantly, or not at all. Of my grandmother, who had died before he sailed for America, he would say only that in her heart she had remained loyal to the Catholic Church and the Stuarts. Nor would he tell me why he had forsaken the proud name of Macduveen for Logan, or why he had left that castle looking toward Skye—first for London, where he had lived for seven years as a very young man, and then for this Long Island village. When I questioned him, all he would say was, "Someday I will explain it to you."

But I felt I knew at least part of the answer. Even though he paid his share of the rates to support our Presbyterian minister, and even attended the Sunday services in the Meeting House a few times each year, perhaps he, like his mother, was at heart a Catholic. One thing was certain. He was fervently loyal to the Stuart cause. As a seventeen-year-old he had joined other Highlanders in their attempt to oust "that Dutchman, George First," from the British throne, and put in his place the "rightful" king, the son of exiled James Second. It was after that rebellion of 1715 had been crushed at the Battle of Preston, I felt sure, that my father, as Walter Logan, had slipped across the border to England, spent seven years in London— where, he told me, he had "made money on the Exchange"—and then, finally, had sailed across the ocean to become a schoolmaster in this sleepy little village.

During my childhood and early girlhood he did not talk of his Jacobite sentiments to the villagers. That would have been unwise. So far the village had tolerated his drinking and his gallant manners, but talk of a Stuart restoration it would not tolerate. And so it was only to me that he spoke of Stuarts, usually on those few evenings when he did not go to the tavern. We would sit at the pine table in the candlelit kitchen, I with my knitting, he with a brandy bottle near his elbow, and he would talk of those

6

royal exiles in faraway Rome. The elder Stuart, the one Jacobites like my father called James Third, and Hanoverians called the Pretender, felt too crushed by his defeat in 1715 to lead another uprising. But his son, Prince Charles Edward, was growing up. "And they say he is a fine lad, handsome even for a Stuart, and with that fiery Stuart courage in his heart."

I did not know why, but such talk filled me with a shadowy foreboding. No matter how warm the night, I would have a sense of chill wind creeping into the room, bending the candle flame, and rattling the copper pans which, after washing up the supper things, I had hung above the hearth. And so I would say, "Father, tell me about Bowain Castle."

"But, Bess, my darling. You should know about the Stuarts. An educated person should be conversant with politics, and I am raising you to be an educated young lady."

That was true. In a village where most women, even women of property, signed their names with an X, I had read the Bible, and Spenser, and Shakespeare, and all my father's books, with the exception of ones like Rabelais and the plays of Plautus and Terence, which he kept locked in the parlor highboy. But somehow my education made me no more eager to hear of the Stuarts and their attendant lords and ladies in that Roman palace, plotting to land again on Scotland's friendly coast and rally the Highlanders and their terrible broadswords. "It is just that I would rather hear about you, Father, when you were a boy in Bowain Castle."

He would sigh. "I suppose I cannot expect a girl child— Very well, Elizabeth. Have I told you about that round tower, standing on a rise about three miles from Bowain Castle? It is very old. No one knows how old, but it was certainly standing there two hundred years ago when the Macduveens wrested those lands from a branch of Clan MacDonald. A woman holding a torch is said to appear from time to time on its parapet, but only to the eyes of those of true Macduveen blood. I never saw her, but the story is that she appeared to the second laird of Bowain Castle and, a century later, to his great-grandson."

He would continue talking, pausing now and then to tip more brandy into his glass. As his face grew more flushed, the sword scar on his forehead, a relic of that battle in which he fought for the Stuarts, would appear whiter. After a while his speech would become thick, and his fine dark eyes would take on a blurred look. I would know that soon he would rise unsteadily, take a candle from the mantelpiece, hold its wick to the flame of the candle on the table, and carry it up to bed, leaving me to bar the door and, if the night had been chill, bank the fire in the hearth. And so I would say, hoping that this time the answer would be different, "Father, will you ever take me to Bowain Castle?"

Always that question seemed to sober him a little. He would look at me, his thin face holding not only sorrow, but what seemed a puzzling guilt. "Perhaps," he would say, in a tone that meant "Never."

But he did take me there, in my eighteenth year. It was a year which began as the most joyous I had lived until then, and toward its midpoint became the bleakest, devoid of any hope except the grim one of staying alive until my nineteenth birthday.

Two

The reason my eighteenth year began so joyously was that, less than a week after my birthday in late January, I fell in love.

Perhaps it would be more apt to say that I discovered that I loved. I had known John Harwood as long as I could remember. When I was seven and he a tall lad of fourteen, he had become one of my father's pupils. Even then, with his dark good looks and quiet manners, he had seemed different from the other pupils, most of them rude, noisy creatures whom I considered unworthy of my father's teaching. Perhaps in part my opinion of John was a reflection of my father's, for the Harwood boy was a favorite of his, too. I later realized that his reason was not just John's own qualities, but his ancestry. He was a direct descendant of an earlier John Harwood—a man of learning and a gentleman, with estates in England—who with several men from Massachusetts Colony had come to Long Island nearly a hundred years before to found the town of Southampton.

Such considerations bear no weight, of course, with a

9

small girl. What won my heart was the sight of John, one day when I was eight, climbing a ladder to rescue my cat Deborah from an oak branch.

Even after he left my father's classes, I of course saw him frequently—in the Meeting House on Sunday, across the gallery partition which separated the young men and boys from the women and girls, and sometimes on weekdays moving down the village's wide Main Street. Frequently I saw him working beside his father in the Harwood fields, because in our village almost every able-bodied person, no matter how rich, works with his hands.

When he was nineteen, he entered Yale College. But whenever the college was not in session, I still caught glimpses of him—seemingly taller and more broad-shouldered each year—as he sat on an oak bench in the Meeting House, or rode a gray gelding along the dusty lanes which wind past farmhouses to the sea.

After his graduation from Yale, he spent two years as a law clerk for a Boston firm. Thus he was in his twenty-fifth year that Sunday morning, four days after my eighteenth birthday, when he fell into step beside me as I went up the snowy Meeting House path. I looked up and met his gaze.

Always I had known that I, with my mother's fair hair and blue eyes, was not unpleasant to look at. But John's dark eyes were saying that he found my appearance much more than pleasant. He asked, faint wonder in his voice, "Elizabeth Logan?"

In my own heart, too, I felt an unfolding wonder. I said, aware that I sounded somewhat breathless, "Yes, John, I am still Elizabeth."

Without speaking again, we went into the Meeting

House. He did not climb the stairs with me to the gallery. He was a man fully grown now, and educated to follow the law, and therefore entitled to sit with the more important men of the community on the front benches. But twice during that long sermon, John turned his head to look up at me.

As I had hoped, I found him waiting when I emerged from the Meeting House. All his family waited—his tall, gray-haired father, his still-handsome mother, and his pretty nineteen-year-old sister Anne—in a group beside the doorway. John said something to them, walked over to me, and asked, "May I see you to your house?"

With his family moving a discreet few yards behind us, we set off through the Sabbath hush. I believe that we talked of the law office he intended to open above the grain merchant's store, but I am not sure. For me the important dialogue was the unspoken one. As we neared my father's saltbox house, its weathered shingles shining like gray satin in the cold sunlight, I asked, "Will you have dinner with us? I am afraid the mutton joint is not large enough for your parents and sister too, but if—"

"I will tell them."

He walked back to the others and spoke briefly. They nodded, smiled at me, and turned back toward Main Street. By the time John rejoined me, I was regretting my invitation. Sometimes alone in the house on Sundays, my father drank. What if we found him at the kitchen table, head pillowed on his crossed arms, and a rum bottle at his elbow?

From its founding, Southampton has always been less severe in church matters than the towns of Massachusetts Bay Colony. Differing religious views, and even a lack of any views, are tolerated. Thus a townsman's nonattendance at church carries no official penalties, as long as he pays his share of the church rates. But our laws designed to preserve the Sabbath's decorum are strict indeed. Fines are levied for "going noisily abroad in the streets," or for riding horseback, except to and from church. And gambling or drinking spirits on Sunday, even in one's home, are legal offenses.

To make matters worse, it was no ordinary young man walking beside me. His father, William Harwood, was chief of the town's Board of Magistrates, that all-powerful board which decided the fate of miscreants like my father.

But at least on that particular afternoon, I need not have worried. Evidently my father had seen us through the window, because as we came up the walk between the leafless privet hedges, the door opened and he stood there, erect, clear-eyed, and with a smile that acknowledged pleasure, but no surprise, that the son of the town's most prominent citizen had escorted his daughter home from church.

The men greeted each other. I hung my hooded cloak on its hook in the hall, hurried back to the kitchen, and covered my best brown linsey with a blue apron. While I moved swiftly about the kitchen, laying pewter plates on the oak table, and fetching the cold joint and yesterday's baked bread from the pantry, I could hear the deep rumble of John's voice in the parlor, and my father's lighter voice, speaking in the cultivated tones that so irritated some of the townspeople.

After dinner we all three sat in the parlor. "Next week, John," my father said, "you will have reason to wish you were still one of my pupils. They are to receive a holiday.

On Tuesday I will sail for Boston."

I was not surprised. The cuffs of his bottle-green great-coat were frayed. Only that morning I had seen him surveying them with distaste. I looked at John, sitting there in his sober black coat and breeches. Perhaps during his years in Boston he, too, had patronized a tailor. But here he dressed like other Southampton men—in homespun.

His dark gaze turned to me. "And you, Elizabeth? You will not stay alone in this house next week, will you?"

My father answered for me. "Elizabeth always stays with Mrs. Fairmont when I am away. Her sons are pupils of mine, you know."

"Could she stay instead with my family? I am sure my mother would be pleased to have her."

My heartbeats quickened. "He wastes no time," I thought. And surely his mother would invite me. If she favored a betrothal between John and me, she would want to test my housewifely skills. If she already disapproved, she would hope to observe flaws in me which she could point out to her son. The latter might well be the case, I realized anxiously. Talk in the village was that she would welcome Charity Clayman as a daughter-in-law. Charity, daughter of another town magistrate, was plain and too thin, but she had a gentle sweetness which might make any woman consider her a desirable wife for her son.

My father gave that pleased but not surprised smile. "Elizabeth?"

It was me that John wanted, not Charity. I need not fear his mother. "If Mrs. Harwood is willing to have me," I said.

That week in the Harwood house was a pleasant one, and not just because John sat across the supper table from

13

me each evening, and slept in a room down the hall from my own. Much larger than our house, and of two stories in the rear as well as the front, the Harwood house sat on a hillside overlooking its own broad acres, now brown with stubble. The Harwoods used earthenware plates for everyday rather than pewter, and a corner cupboard in the kitchen held real china, brought from England by the first John Harwood.

I helped Mrs. Harwood and Anne card wool that week, and dip candles. I took my turn at the spinning wheel, and at the heavy loom in the lean-to off the kitchen. Several times I saw approval in Mrs. Harwood's face, and once she said, "I had thought, a girl with only a father— But your mother taught you well, Elizabeth, and you have remembered."

On my last day there, as we sat in the candlelit parlor after our five o'clock supper, Mrs. Harwood got to her feet, lit another candle from the row on the mantelpiece, and said, "Come, William. Come, Anne. I want to speak to you in the kitchen."

Their footsteps died away down the hall. For perhaps a minute John and I sat in silence, I on the oak settle with its quilted cushion, my eyes cast down, he in a ladderback chair opposite me. Then he said, "Elizabeth, I wish to speak to your father. Have I your permission?"

I raised my gaze. At the look on his handsome face—his dark eyes confident, but his smile showing a trace of anxiety—I forgot my intention to appear to hesitate. "You have, John." I added, even more boldly, "And I am sure he will favor you."

He rose, drew me to my feet, and kissed me. "We will live here at first," he said, "but later we will build our own

14

house on Harwood land. There is plenty of room."

I looked up at his face, lighted with the happiness I felt in my own heart. And then suddenly I thought of Bowain Castle, looking across the strait toward Skye. With an inward shiver I thought how fortunate it was that I had never realized my childish desire to go there to live, that instead I had stayed here, until John Harwood's eyes and heart had turned toward me.

The next afternoon, John and his sister walked with me the two miles to my house. Less than an hour after I bade them good-bye, Jeb Olmstead, the carter who carried goods and passengers from the habor at North Sea, stopped his wagon before our gate. Standing at the window, I watched my father get down and brush dust from the sleeves of a new, dark blue greatcoat. As he started up the walk, I saw that his fawn breeches were also new, and that he had ornamented his old beaver tricorn with a white cockade. I rushed to the door and opened it.

He kissed me. "Well, Elizabeth, did you enjoy your stay with the esteemed Harwoods?"

"Oh, yes!" I had smelled rum on his breath. But I sensed it was more than drink which had brought that glow to his eyes. He had the look of a man bursting with some tremendous news.

Arm around my waist, he walked back to the kitchen with me. There I faced him and said, "Father, I have given John Harwood permission to speak to you."

"Upon what subject?"

"Father! Please don't tease."

"All right, my poppet." He kissed me again and then said, "It is a good match. And an even better match for John than it is for you. I hope he realizes that."

He paused. "And now for my news." He drew a deep breath. "Elizabeth, he has landed! He raised the Stuart standard at Glenfinnan last July!"

I said dazedly, "Father, I don't—"

"Where are your wits, girl? Prince Charles has come to Scotland to put his father on the throne. The clans have rallied to him, and— But here. Read it for yourself."

Reaching inside his new greatcoat, he brought out a one-page Boston newspaper and handed it to me. Large print across the top said, "Tremendous Happenings in Britain." I skimmed the columns of print. Landed in the Highlands in July—Defeated the English at Prestopans—French troops expected to come to his support. The newspaper's account ended, "Our latest intelligence is that the English troops have fled from the old Scottish capital of Edinburgh, leaving Prince Charles and his Highland troops in control."

My father had begun to pace up and down. "French support or no French support, Prince Charles will beat any troops the English send against him. And then he will chase Fat George back to Hanover, where he belongs. Here, read this."

He had taken printed handbills from inside his coat. Sick with dismay, I read the one he gave me: "Men of Southampton! Declare your loyalty to your rightful king. Down with the usurper, the Elector of Hanover, who miscalls himself King George the Second. Long live James the Third, King of England and Scotland, and his son and heir, Prince Charles Edward!"

"Father, did you—"

"Of course I had them printed in Boston." He opened the cupboard and took down a bottle and a glass. Lifting the filled glass, he said, "To Bonnie Prince Charlie!" He downed half the glass's contents. "I heard in Boston that they call him that."

"Father, you must not show those handbills in Southampton. It is—sedition."

"Sedition? Have I not proved to you again and again that the throne belongs to the Stuarts?"

"I don't care about that!" I cried wildly. "No one here cares about that!"

I felt that was true. Southampton people had no great love of George the Second. They grumbled at his taxes, and cheated the crown whenever possible by smuggling goods ashore, duty-free, on Long Island's beaches. But they had even less love of the Stuarts. After all, the Stuarts were Catholics, and our village is overwhelmingly Protestant. Mainly, of course, Southampton people wanted to live and work in peace, undisturbed by the warring factions of the Britain they or their ancestors had fled.

Banishment, I thought. The town might banish him. Under its charter, Southampton could vote for the expulsion of any freeman in its midst, provided it compensated him for land or other property he left behind. Several times during the colony's hundred years of existence, Southampton men had exercised that right.

"They will banish you," I said. And what then, I thought, of John and me? What then?

"Banish me? Ha! If they did, how would they get their thick-headed sons into Yale? Surely not by sending them to the village school!" He restored the bottle to the cupboard. "Well, don't wait supper for me."

I clutched his arm. "You are not going to the tavern!

Not with those handbills!"

"Child, child! Don't you see that Charles is winning? 'There is a tide in the affairs of men, which, taken at the flood, leads on to fortune.' Not all men here know Shakespeare, but they know what it means to be on the winning side. Besides, there are others here of Highland ancestry. Bruce McNab, for instance. You will see how my news sets them on fire; you will see."

He went down the hall. I heard the door open and close. There was something final in the sound, as if he were shutting me away from all the happy years that, less than an hour ago, had seemed so inevitable.

Three

It took the town almost a month to lose patience with my father.

Perhaps he had been correct in thinking that his knowledge of Latin and Greek made him almost indispensable. Perhaps the fact that his daughter was betrothed to the son of Southampton's most prominent citizen helped save him. Or perhaps some of the townspeople, although certainly not all, discovered that they were proud of this peacock in their sober midst.

Whatever its reasons, the town at first contented itself with warnings. The handbills my father had nailed to trees and fence posts were taken down, and the magistrates sent him written notice not to "offend the public peace" in such a manner again. One Sunday our minister preached a sermon against those "who would sow strife amongst us." My father was not there to hear it, but I was, helplessly aware that even though I held my head high, color flamed in my face. Responsible men of the community, like William and John Harwood, tried to argue my father out of his obsession. Several times when

John had supper with us, I lingered in the kitchen afterwards, listening to the sound of John's earnest voice in the parlor, and my father's—at first quietly argumentative, then cuttingly amused, as if John were still a lad in his classroom, and then, finally, so loud and enraged that I hurried down the hall to the parlor, knowing that my entrance would stop their quarrel.

But neither argument nor warning availed. Each night my father went to the tavern. As I waited at home, picturing him surrounded by fellow townsmen—some grave, some angry, some jeeringly amused—I thanked heaven that our community was too small and isolated to merit policing by the King's soldiers. If this had been Boston or Philadelphia, my father long since would have been arrested.

One morning almost three weeks after his return from Boston, he as usual laid out his books on the parlor desk, and moved out from the wall the long table, scarred by initials carved with penknives, at which his pupils sat. Eight o'clock passed, nine. No boys came up the walk.

That seemed to frighten him. He stayed indoors all day, most of the time staring out the parlor window, and that night after supper he did not go to the tavern, but sat at his desk, Caesar's *Commentaries* open before him, and no bottle at his elbow. The next day, and the next, and the next, the parlor remained empty of pupils. And each evening, cold sober, he went to bed soon after supper.

My spirits brightened somewhat. Soon he would go to the magistrates, apologize, and promise not to offend again. His pupils would return. And when John and I talked of our marriage in the spring, I would no longer see worry in his eyes, or feel it weighting my own heart.

One Monday afternoon my father left the house for the first time in five days. He did not return for supper. Around eight-thirty, just as I was about to enter my bedroom, the front door opened and closed. I heard the scrape of the flint box we kept on a table in the lower hall. Then he came up the stairs, his face taut with excitement in the glow of the candle he carried. Even before he was close enough for me to smell the rum, I knew that he had been drinking. "Father, were you—"

"I was not at the tavern, my poppet. I was at North Sea."

A boat must have come into the harbor there, probably a boat from Boston.

"Great news, Elizabeth." How exuberant he looked, and how young. " 'There is a tide—' And it is running strong now."

My heart contracted. "What do you mean?"

"You will know in the morning. Everyone will know. Go to bed, Daughter."

The next morning William Harwood himself tore down the handbill that my father, under cover of darkness, had affixed to the notice board outside the Meeting House. I never saw the handbill. By the time that I, after an almost sleepless night, hurried through a light snowfall to the center of the village, the handbill had been taken down. The few men and women clustered around the board turned away, with embarrassed faces, at my approach. Only Dick McNab, a loutish fifteen-year-old whom my father recently had expelled for insolence, waited for me, grinning. The handbill, he told me, had said that now the Prince was across the English border. Carlisle had fallen to him without a shot being fired. The handbill had concluded with the exhortation to "overthrow the Dutch usurper, and rally around your rightful King."

Filled with anxiety and humiliation, I hurried down Job's Lane. If John had been at home, I would have walked to the Harwood house for comfort and counsel. But the day before John and several other young men had sailed a sloop across the Sound to buy plowshares from the foundry in Connecticut. They would not return until the next day. And without John's stalwart and loving presence, I could not face his family.

That afternoon the Board of Magistrates' clerk brought my father written notice to appear the next day before the Town Meeting.

When the door had closed behind the clerk, my father turned to me a pale but determinedly optimistic face. "It is better this way. Now I can state King James's case before every freeman in town. And I am sure that my argument will prevail."

Not speaking, I turned toward the kitchen to make supper. What could one say to a man so sure of the righteousness of his cause that he believed, against all evidence, that he could convince others?

Although I knew he must be back from Connecticut, John did not come to me the next day. His absence, although disappointing, neither surprised nor frightened me. I knew that just as my father, bent over foolscap in the parlor, was preparing his defense, so John—and his father, too, I hoped—must be busy trying to persuade the townspeople to be lenient toward the misguided man who would appear before them.

My father spent all morning writing his speech. He did not offer to let me read it, nor did I ask to, but I knew what must be in it—a genealogy of the exiled James Stuart, tracing his line back through James Second and the two Charleses to James First, and then even farther back to the Tudor kings. His speech would be logical, impassioned, and perhaps incontrovertible. And it would move these Long Island farmers and craftsmen and merchants not one whit. Only men like William and John Harwood could do that.

At dinner, a meal scarcely touched by either of us, my father said, "You are not to come to the Meeting House."

Was he, then, less confident than he pretended? "I am coming with you."

"Elizabeth, you will obey me!" Never before had he spoken to me that sharply. He added, in a gentler tone, "It is not that I am afraid. It is that long face of yours. One look at it, and people will feel that my own daughter is convinced that I should be hung on Tyburn Hill."

Tyburn Hill! I wanted to scream at him, "There's no Tyburn here. This is Long Island, Father. *Long Island!*"

A little before two o'clock he set off up the lane, swinging the blackthorn stick he had bought several years before in Boston. I sat in the parlor, hands tightly clenched, eyes going repeatedly to the hourglass on the mantelpiece. The charge must have been read by now. What evidence was being given against him? What was John and, pray God, John's father, saying in his defense?

At last I could bear it no longer. I put on my cloak, left the house, and hurried up Job's Lane. There was no one else in sight, and I knew that was not just because of the lowering sky and a wind that smelled of coming snow. For freemen of Southampton, attendance at Town Meeting was compulsory. And today the women, except for those

23

too old, or sick, or with very young children, would have climbed the stairs to the gallery.

I entered the Meeting House vestibule, struggling to keep the wind from slamming the heavy door behind me. The vestibule was murky, lighted by only one candle in its sconce above the closed inner doors. From beyond them came a high-pitched voice I recognized. The speaker was Bruce McNab, descendant of Highlanders, nightly tippler at the tavern, and father of the boy my father had expelled. I climbed to the gallery.

At my entrance there was a rustle among the rows of women and young boys, and a turning of heads. Looking straight before me, I descended the steps along the partition toward a front bench. Now I could hear McNab's voice clearly. "—night after night, spouting balderdash about King James and Bonnie Prince Charlie. Again and again I said to him, 'Logan, if you don't hold your tongue, you'll bring Redcoats here.' But nothing will stop that blatherskate. So mark my words—"

The rustling in the gallery must have reached his ears. Breaking off, McNab looked up to where I had sat down on the front bench. John Harwood, sitting three benches from the front, had turned to look up, his expression unreadable in the mingled, uncertain illumination of wall candles and of gray daylight filtering through the windows. William Harwood, seated at the long magistrates' table which faced the rows of benches, had raised his gaze to me. And my father, seated alone beyond the benches at a small oak table provided for those accused, had not only looked up, but had gotten to his feet. Strained face upturned to mine, he mouthed the words "Go home."

I shook my head.

William Harwood, gray hair shining in the dim light, face set in unhappy but purposeful lines, rapped his gavel. My father, after one more imploring look at me, sat down and faced the magistrates.

McNab, his face now flushed beneath his carroty hair, resumed speaking. "Maybe some of you feel sorry for Walter Logan, and I wager we all feel sorry for his daughter. But sense is sense. If he goes on like this, we'll have the King's soldiers snooping over our farms, and interfering with our trade"—with your smuggling, you mean, I thought bitterly—"and maybe hauling off innocent men. That is all I have to say."

He sat down. My heart ached for my father, so learned in Latin and Greek, so blindly ignorant of human nature. How could he have believed that McNab's Highland ancestry would count in the least against his self-interest as a Southampton man, let alone his grudge over his son's expulsion?

Mr. Harwood said, "Have any others evidence to give against the accused?" He waited. No one stirred. "Does anyone wish to speak in favor of the accused?"

I fixed my gaze on the back of John's dark head. He would rise now. I did not know exactly what he would say. Perhaps he would plead that to any fair-minded man there was at least some justice in the cause my father preached. Probably he would remind them of my father's value to the community. And surely he would plead that, even if they found my father guilty, they should mete out some lesser punishment, such as putting him under bond to insure that he no longer disturbed and endangered his fellow townsmen.

Seconds passed. John did not rise.

I felt myself turning cold, as if from a numbing blow from a trusted hand. I heard William Harwood say, "Then we will vote. Who finds Walter Logan guilty as charged?"

Gaze fixed on John's back, I was aware of hands going up all around him.

His hand went up.

Through a faint roaring in my ears, I heard William Harwood ask, "Who among you finds Walter Logan not guilty?"

If a hand went up, and I am sure none did, I did not see it. My unbelieving gaze was still fixed on the man with whom I had expected to live until I died.

"Walter Logan, do you have anything to say before your sentence is voted upon?"

My father rose, the pages of foolscap rustling in his hand. He turned toward the gallery. This time he did not mouth the words. He said clearly, "Go home, Elizabeth." His white face seemed to swim up toward me through the murky light. "Go home, Daughter."

I got to my feet. As I stumbled up the aisle, a woman reached her hand out to me. It was Charity Clayman, her thin, plain face filled with compassion. But I was too stricken to accept the comfort she offered. I brushed past her hand and went through the doorway and down the stairs. Through the vestibule's doors I could hear my father reading the carefully prepared speech that would sway his hearers not one bit. Only the man I had loved could hope to sway them. And he had not even raised his hand, let alone spoken a word, to defend my father.

I waited for nearly an hour in our parlor while the first fat snowflakes spiraled down outside, and the tiny windowpanes, as the dark thickened beyond them, became increasingly bright mirrors for the candle burning on the mantelpiece. At last the front door opened and closed.

My father came in, brushing snow from the sleeves of his fine new coat. His face was pale, but his smile looked cheerful, even gay. "It is settled. I no longer will spend my days pounding Greek into dullards, and my evenings drinking with their thick-headed fathers."

So it was banishment. I had thought that after all they might vote some lesser punishment, such as a heavy fine, to be paid either in cash or by labor on the town roads and the fence enclosing the common. But I was just as glad it was banishment. There was nothing left for me here. "How soon must we leave?"

"We? You are not banished, Daughter. You will stay here, as John's wife." He smiled teasingly. "Or had you forgotten you were pledged?"

Did he really believe that today had not altered my whole future as well as his own? No, he did not believe that. Despite his unruffled air, I could see guilt and sorrow deep in his eyes. "You know I cannot marry John."

"Why not? The Harwoods are honorable men. They did as conscience dictated."

I perceived that I did not have to explain why, after today, I could not marry John, and live with him, and bear his children. My father already realized that I could not. Now, when it was too late, he realized that. "No, I will not marry him."

After a moment he said briskly, "Perhaps it is just as well. Yale College or no Yale College, he is not good enough for you. What would you say to a landed knight as a husband, or even a belted earl? Yes, why not an earl?"

Had he taken leave of his senses entirely? Where in Connecticut, or whatever place might take us in, would we find an earl, belted or unbelted? I repeated, "How soon must we leave?"

"They voted a fortnight."

Two weeks in which to sell our house. "What price do you think we can get for our house? Enough to buy another in Connecticut?"

"I am afraid not, Daughter." Spots of color had appeared on his cheekbones. "I did not want to worry you, but three years ago I had to borrow money from Harry Jackson." Jackson, a farmer and harness maker, already owned several houses in the village. In my mind's eye I could see him sitting behind and a little to the right of John that afternoon, could see his hand shooting up when William Harwood called for the guilty votes.

"I pledged the house to him. And therefore, since I have been unable to repay the loan . . ."

Debt. That was how he had been able to buy fine clothes, and go to the tavern almost every night. And now we had nothing! For a terrible moment I felt hatred for my father. The emotion passed. I loved him, and not just for his learning and his good looks and his tenderness toward me. I loved him for the very qualities—fastidiousness in dress, gallantry of manner, and fervent loyalty to his cause—which had brought us to disaster.

"Then we have no money at all?"

"Enough for our passage."

"Passage!"

"To Scotland."

After a moment I realized it was probably the best solution. At least we had kin there.

28

Or did we? He had mentioned that at the time he left Bowain Castle his Uncle James Macduveen and his wife, although married for several years, had no children. And by now perhaps they themselves . . .

"Do you know if your uncle and his wife are still alive?"

His face took on a closed look. "No."

"Were they alive when you left England for the Colonies?"

"I don't know." His gaze slid away from mine. "I neither saw them nor heard anything of them after I went down to London. I have told you that."

He had not. He had told me almost nothing of his London years.

"Even if the laird and his wife are still alive, will we be welcome at Bowain Castle? You have never actually said so, but I have felt there was bad blood between yourself and your uncle."

"Don't concern yourself with it, Bess. For a while I will leave you with some respectable family in Glasgow. You will like Glasgow. Defoe called it the fairest town in Britain."

"*Leave* me there?"

"Yes. I will be with the Prince's forces."

Too astonished to speak, I looked at the sword scar across his forehead, that souvenir of his services to the elder Stuart. But the Battle of Preston was now thirty years in the past.

"I know," he said. "I am a bit long in the tooth to wield a claymore. But royalty always find use for a man of learning. And they say that the Prince is as warm-hearted as he is brave. He will be grateful to a man who crosses the ocean to serve him.

"And think, Daughter. You will see Scotland. Remember how, as a little lass, you used to beg me to take you to Scotland to live?"

But I was no longer a little lass. I was a woman who had loved a man, and who might find, once this numb shock wore off, that she still loved him. And then how many years would pass before I would cease to think of that house we would never build, those children we would never have?

Despite my best efforts, my voice sounded flat and bleak. "Yes, Father. I have always wanted to see Scotland."

Four

The *Prudence*, three weeks out of Boston and wrapped in fog, was not becalmed, but almost so. As I stood in the darkness of the midship deck, back to the rail, I could see by the fog-blurred glow of the mainmast lantern that the mainsail went slack every once in a while, flapped idly, and then, as the fitful breeze filled it, grew taut. In the ship's bow, visible to me whenever the fog thinned, the lookout every few minutes tolled a warning bell.

It was chill on deck, and the bell's tolling oppressed me. Still, I wanted to delay as long as possible my descent to the cabin I shared with three other women—one of them seasick ever since we left Boston Harbor—and with a colicky infant. On deck I could at least draw clean air into my lungs.

I looked to my left. Several yards away, nearer to the lookout in the bow than to me, my father stood hunched at the rail, staring down at the fog-shrouded water.

A change had come over him during the past week. All through those last strained days in Southampton, he had remained cheerful. He was even gallant to the housewives who came up the walk to bargain for our pewter and our pots and pans and featherbeds. (With grim satisfaction, I noticed that their husbands lacked the courage to bargain for the goods of the man they had banished.) Later on, while we waited in our cramped Boston lodgings to secure passage on a ship, he remained in good spirits. Each day he went down to the docks to see if some ship had brought fresh news of the fighting. Often he would return flushed with triumph. The Prince and his Highlanders were still moving toward London, elusive as foxes when they wished to avoid King George's armies, and terrible as lions when they chose to give battle. "They say he is striking for Derby," he told me on one such day. "And Derby, my poppet, is not much more than a hundred and fifty miles from London! I will wager that by now Fat George has loaded a few ships with his valuables, ready to run back to Hanover."

When we finally secured passage on the *Prudence*, in the cheapest accommodations possible, his high spirits persisted. "It will be for only a few weeks, Bess. And this time next year you may be dining at the Court of St. James. How does that sit with you, Lady Elizabeth?"

Lady Elizabeth, wife of that titled gentleman he seemed to expect me to marry. I, who by this time should have been Mrs. John Harwood. Perhaps he saw the pain in my eyes, because he said hastily, "You had best get your sleep. We sail on the morning tide."

During our first days aboard the *Prudence*, his cheerfulness did not flag. At meals the passengers shared with the ship's officers, he spoke enthusiastically of the Stuart cause. His hearers, unlike the men of Southampton, responded either noncommittally or with cautious agreement. Apparently my father had been right about one thing. Most people did want to be on the winning side. And King George, with his best troops away fighting in Austria and his home troops scattering before the Highlanders and their two-handed sword which could sever an arm with one slash, seemed fated to lose.

During the third week of our voyage, as we moved sluggishly under skies that even now, in mid-May, often had the leaden look of winter, my father began to change. He said less and less at meals. Often, sensing his gaze, I would turn to look at him, only to have him look away. After our evening meal of tea and salted beef and hard biscuits, he did not linger at table to drink with the men passengers and off-duty officers. Instead, with a fresh bottle of rum purchased from the ship's stores, he would climb the companionway to stand at the rail in the darkness.

For a few nights I had tried to stand beside him, but although he did not tell me to leave him, his averted gaze and brief replies made it plain he preferred solitude. What was it that weighed upon him? Now that Scotland was only about ten days away—less, given favorable winds— had he begun to feel dark premonitions? Or was he aware that, contrary to the hope he must have had, I was no nearer to forgetting John than I had been when I left Southampton?

John. Turning, I looked down over the rail at a patch of water, black beneath a rift in the fog. But in my mind's eye I saw John's face as it had looked at our last meeting.

At almost nine o'clock that night, six hours after he had voted to find my father guilty, he knocked on the door. My father had gone upstairs by then. Perhaps he had expected John to call, and had considered it fair to give him

33

every opportunity to plead his case. I opened the door. John's face was pale and unsmiling. "I know this is an unseemly hour, but I must see you."

Unseemly! I felt a wild impulse to laugh in his face. After what he had done that afternoon, I wondered that he could even use the word. "Come in," I said coldly.

In the parlor we faced each other. "Tell me, will your father have sufficient funds?"

I said, in that same cold voice, "I don't know what you mean by sufficient. Certainly he has very little, since this house is pledged for debt."

From his expression I realized that he had known that. Perhaps everyone but me had known it. He said, "I would like to loan him fifty pounds. With that sum he can make a fresh start almost anywhere he chooses."

My heart began to pound. "Do you think that my father would accept your money?"

"Why not? You and I can be wed sooner than we planned." Despite his matter-of-fact tone, the bleakness of his eyes told me that he had guessed my decision. "A man cannot object to borrowing money from his son-in-law."

"You think that you will become his son-in-law? After you voted for his banishment? What sort of a mean, poor-spirited creature do you think I am?"

"Elizabeth!" He caught my hands. I pulled them free. He said, his own hands dropping to his sides, "It is compulsory for every freeman to vote. And once the charge was made, how could I, trained to know the law and sworn to uphold it, find him other than guilty? Your father talks treason, Elizabeth. He has for weeks now."

"You could have argued for a lesser punishment!"

"A fine? Not without making a travesty of the law. Fines are for slanderers and Sabbath-breakers, not for a man whose seditious talk has endangered a whole community. But surely he has learned today the necessity of restraint. If so, with his abilities, he will fare well enough, wherever he goes."

I knew he would not, not unless I was with him, to curb at least some of his extravagant behavior, and to see to it that he was supplied with nourishing food as well as rum.

John again caught my hands. This time I allowed them to lie cold and unresponsive in his grasp. "Elizabeth, don't ruin both our lives. We are suited. Neither of us will ever find anyone to suit us so well. We are bound to each other. If you send me away, you will learn that."

I said flatly, "I cannot marry you."

After a moment he released my hands. "Very well. I will be back tomorrow. We will talk of it then."

"The door will not be open to you."

"Nevertheless, I will come back."

He did come back the next day, in the early afternoon and again after dark. He came up our walk the following afternoon, too. Each time I did not answer his knock. Nor did my father urge me to. Instead he looked at me with conflicting emotions plain in his eyes, guilt over my broken betrothal, and an irrepressible gladness that I was to come with him.

John Harwood did not return to our house a fourth time. For his sake, as well as my own, I was glad. A man like John Harwood should humble himself only so far to regain a woman.

I had hoped that time and distance would dull my need

for him. But it was as sharp as ever. Often at night in that
noxious cabin, kept awake by snores that ceased only
when the baby awoke screaming, I would remember that
by now I should be lying in an upstairs room of the Harwood house, with John's arms around me. Then I would
fold the rough pillow over my face to muffle my sobs, and
weep until a dull exhaustion crept over me.

A movement of my father's caught my eye. I turned my
head and saw him lift the bottle to his lips. My fastidious
father who in the past, no matter how drunk, had
always measured his rum out deliberately and lifted his
glass as if to admire its color before he took the first swallow. He kept his head tilted back for perhaps two seconds.
Then, the bottle still in his hand, he leaned over the rail,
with coughs racking his body. He had been coughing for
at least two weeks now, and he had grown much thinner.
It was just that he ate so little, I told myself, trying to
silence a growing alarm in my heart. Once we were
ashore, free of the ship's constant motion and with palat-
able food spread before us, he would be himself again.

I walked to the companionway and descended to that
crowded cabin.

Five

On a bright June morning, the *Prudence* angled across the Clyde River toward her mooring wharf. Beside me at the rail, my father stared at the tall warehouses along the river's edge. Recalling his description of Glasgow—the pretty houses, the sheep grazing beneath giant oaks in the meadows that bordered the river—I could understand the stunned look on his face.

The first mate, a tall man from Concord, stopped beside us. "Well, Mr. Logan, here we are."

My father said, "It is hard to believe that this is Glasgow." He looked down at the river flotsam—barrels coated with tar, a bundle of broom straw, a fragment of moldy bread that sank even as we watched. "And it is hard to believe that this used to be one of the best salmon rivers in Britain."

The first mate chuckled. "Glasgow men have little time for fishing now. Tobacco, Mr. Logan, tobacco from the American colonies. That is what makes Glasgow rich. Surely you knew it was now Britain's main tobacco port."

"Yes, but I had not known it had changed the town so

much." He looked apprehensive, as if he had read some evil omen in the befouled river, the long wharf swarming with blue-clad dockhands, and the public coaches waiting at the dock's far end. A fit of coughing doubled him over the rail. When he straightened, he said, "Get your portmanteau, Elizabeth."

My cabin mates were already on deck. For the first time since we left Boston, I had the dark, ill-smelling hole to myself. Perhaps the anxiety in my father's face had communicated itself to me, because my fingers had trouble with the portmanteau straps. When I emerged onto the deck, my father stood at the top of the gangplank, his hand trunk beside him. A sturdy dockhand, a blond man in his twenties, was climbing toward him.

"Shall I carry your baggage, sir?"

"Yes." My father laid his hand on the man's arm. "But first, tell me about the Prince."

The deckhand stared. "Prince? What prince?"

"Don't be dense, man. Charles Edward Stuart, of course."

"Oh, that one." He spat over the rail. "Don't you know? No, I guess you don't, being at sea all that time. Billy took care of *him*, all right."

"Billy?" My father's face had turned gray.

"His Majesty's second son William, the Duke of Cumberland. Smashed Charlie's Highlanders good, Billy did, up near Inverness, at a place called Culloden. Last April it was. No one knows where Charlie is. Maybe the Frenchies sent a ship to take him back where he belongs. Or maybe he's still skulking around up north."

My father said in a thick voice, "You lying Whig scum."

The dockhand laughed. "You must be one of those Jacobite Johnnies. Didn't know they had them in the Colonies. Of course I'm a Whig. So are most of us here in the Lowlands, and plenty in the Highlands too. We've got no use for any Papists, especially Stuarts." He added, scowling now, "And you can carry your own baggage."

His face suddenly old, my father stared after the man's retreating back. I said, not believing my own words, "He was playing a joke on you, Father."

"Shall I help you ashore, Mr. Logan?"

I turned to see a middle-aged man, one of the ship's sailors, standing beside us. Without waiting for an answer, he lifted the trunk with one hand and the portmanteau with the other. We followed him along the crowded dock toward the one remaining coach. At our approach the elderly driver descended from the box, placed my portmanteau inside the coach, and helped the sailor strap the trunk onto the luggage rack.

"Well, good-bye, Mr. Logan, Miss Logan."

My father reached inside his coat and brought out his leather purse. The sailor said, "No need of that, sir." There was pity in his eyes. For my father's cough, and the stains on his coat that betokened a growing carelessness? Or had the sailor, too, heard that the man my father had traveled thousands of miles to join had been defeated at a place called Culloden? "Good luck, Mr. Logan," he added, and walked back toward the ship.

My father said, "Take us to lodgings, please."

From the coachman's expression, I knew that he had observed the thinness of my father's purse. "What sort of lodgings?"

"The more modest, the better." My father's tone told me how hard he found it to say those words.

The coach carried us down an alley between tall warehouses and then along a high street, thronged with carts, public and private coaches, and occasional sedan chairs. Pedestrians, many of them richly dressed, moved along the sidewalks, or stood looking into shop windows. Even the few ragged urchins darting in and out among the strollers looked well-fed. Tobacco had indeed been good to Glasgow.

We turned to our right past a row of close-packed stone houses. The first ones looked well-cared-for, but farther along I saw unscrubbed front steps, smeared windows, and one with rags stuffed into a broken pane. At last the coach stopped before a three-story house with peeling gray paint. The coachman, carrying our baggage, led us up fairly clean steps to the front door. It opened promptly at his knock, and a thin, dark-haired woman of about forty peered out at us.

"I've brought you custom, Mrs. Ludlow. Have you two vacant rooms?"

"After a manner of speaking." Her shrewd gray eyes went from my father to me and then back again. "Your daughter?"

"Yes, madam."

She opened the door wide. "Come in."

We followed her and the coachman up two flights of stairs. She opened the door of a smallish room that contained two narrow beds, a three-legged stool, and a washstand which held a chipped pitcher and basin. She crossed the room, seized a calico curtain suspended from a length of string and drew it between the beds, dividing the room into two unequal portions. "Now it is the same as two rooms. The privy is out back. The price is four shillings a night, with breakfast six pence for each of you."

The price was outrageous, but I hoped my father would not demur. Obviously he needed to lie down, and at once. His face was flushed now, and I feared it was from more than the exertion of climbing stairs.

"Very well, madam." He paid the coachman ten pence and then, when Mrs. Ludlow held out her palm, counted four shillings into it.

When they had left us, my father said, "Wait here for me."

"You cannot go out!" I touched his cheek. It was burning hot. "You are ill. We must find a doctor."

"And have the fool bleed me?"

I did not try to answer that. It was not only his political opinions which had outraged our Southampton neighbors. He flew in the face of respected medical thought too. It was doctors bleeding their already weakened victims, he said, which kept the village gravediggers busy.

"Then at least lie down and rest."

"How can I rest until I know the truth or falsity of what that ruffian told us?"

Yes, it would be impossible for him to rest until he found out. "Very well. But come back as soon as you learn."

When he had gone, I inspected the beds, and found that the sheets, although coarse, appeared clean, and that there seemed to be no fleas or other vermin. After that I changed from my brown woolen dress to a green muslin from my portmanteau, and sat down to wait.

More than an hour must have passed before I heard his slow footsteps on the stairs. I opened the door. One look at his face, and I had no reason to ask if the dockhand had told the truth.

Shoulders hunched, he walked past me to the far side of the room and sank down on the bed. "Rest," I said. "Sleep if you can."

As if I had not spoken, he said, "It is true. Fat George's fat son William beat him. Pray God he escaped to France, but it is not believed that he did. George's soldiers and local militiamen are combing the Highlands for him, and the Western Isles too."

Obviously he would not rest until he had told me his tragic news. I carried the low wooden stool close to his bed and sat down.

"He could have won," my father said. "He marched as far south as Derby, with the dragoons scattering ahead of him like rabbits. A hundred and fifty miles away, London was in panic. People were storming the Bank of England to draw out their money. The royal yachts were at anchor in the Thames, ready to take George and his household back to Hanover. But Charles did not know all that, and so he listened to his commanders."

He fell broodingly silent. After a few moments I prompted, "And?"

"They wanted the Prince to withdraw north of the Scottish border and wait until French troops joined him before making the final assault."

As my father talked on, I could see how the commanders had reached their fatal misjudgment. They had agreed to march deep into England only because they believed that much of the English countryside would join them. It had not. In the small towns and villages through which the victorious Highlanders marched, plaids slung over their shoulders and bagpipes swirling, people had watched them in uneasy or apathetic silence. No wonder the commanders had begun to worry about their estates back in Scotland, left unprotected against English counterassault. Only the common soldiers shared the Prince's passionate conviction that a victorious army does not retreat.

"It must have taken the heart out of them," my father said, "to turn around, with London so close, and march north. In the English towns, even the small boys jeered at them, because they looked like losers now, even though they were not—not yet."

The Prince managed to win two more victories, one of them at Falkirk, where some of the embittered Highlanders gave no quarter to the English wounded, a barbarity that the English were to repay tenfold. For by then the English army, strengthened by troops withdrawn from Austria, was in close pursuit. For the retreating Highlanders, everything seemed to go wrong. Field guns were swept away in river crossings. Supplies arrived so haphazardly that often they went hungry. And on a moor near Inverness, chosen by the Prince for a stand against his pursuers, fortune deserted the Highlanders entirely.

"English cannon killed one man in three before the Highlanders even charged," my father said. "And when they finally did charge, with wind driving icy sleet straight into their faces, English muskets did for most of the rest of them. The few who managed to break through to the English swordsmen beyond found themselves so vastly outnumbered that they had little chance to use their broadswords."

Within ten minutes after that first desperate charge, it was all over. The English, swarming across the battlefield, took their ample revenge for Falkirk. They butchered the wounded Highlanders where they lay, and scoured the nearby fields and ditches and hedgerows for any who might have managed to crawl to temporary safety.

"Since then the English dragoons have been all over the Highlands, burning houses and driving off cattle, and searching for the few men who escaped alive from the battlefield. And for the Prince, of course. I have seen the handbills the English government has issued. They offer thirty thousand pounds to anyone who will 'seize and bind the Pretender, Charles Edward Stuart,' and bring him to justice."

Thirty thousand pounds! It was a vast fortune. If the Prince had not escaped to France, then obviously he had loyal friends throughout the Highlands. Otherwise, someone long since would have collected that reward.

Incredibly, my father was smiling. "The Prince must have kept his high spirits, though. They say that he has offered a one-pound reward for anyone who will seize and bind George, the Elector of Hanover."

His smile vanished. He coughed violently for a few moments, and then rested his face in his hands. For a while I said nothing. What words would have been adequate?

At last I asked, "And you and I, Father? What will we do?"

He took his hands away from his face. "A coach leaves for Inverness tomorrow morning. I have already paid our fare."

"And from Inverness? Are we going to Bowain Castle?"

"Yes," he said after a moment's silence. "I have almost no money, and so there is nothing else to do. We should be able to find some sort of conveyance to take us there, at least a wagon."

Not only reluctance but fear was obvious in his voice and his averted gaze. I said, "I have always felt you never wanted to see Bowain Castle again. Why do you feel that way?"

"I cannot talk about it now. Before we arrive there, I will tell you."

"But don't I—"

"Of course you have a right to know!" His tone was almost fierce. "But your father is a coward, Elizabeth. That is something I have discovered these past few weeks. Now let me rest, Daughter. Let me rest."

Six

The coach lurched. Miss Lucy Phipps, on the seat opposite my father and myself, screamed and fell against the stout man on her right. At the same moment her feet lifted slightly from the floor, revealing the torn ruffle of a green satin petticoat. The stout man laughed. The man on her left, almost equally stout but younger, grasped her arm and drew her to an upright position. "A rough road," he said, "makes for closer acquaintanceship."

The other three passengers already had been seated when my father and I reached the coach yard on Glasgow's high street that morning. The men, both associated with Glasgow tobacco firms, were on their way to Inverness. So was Miss Phipps, a tall, dark-haired woman of about thirty. She came, she told us, from London, where she sang in opera.

But when we were only a mile or so from Glasgow, moving through green pasture land toward low hills, their rounded tops dimly visible through the morning mist, the older of the two men produced a brandy bottle. At first Miss Phipps refused the proffered refreshment. Then suddenly she opened her portmanteau and took out a small silver tumbler. From then on the three of them drank, the men from the bottle, she sipping genteelly from the tumbler the stout man kept filled. And as the banter between the three grew louder and bolder, I came : the unmistakable conclusion that the source of Miss Phipps's income was not singing.

Now she said, "What ails that driver? Laws! I thought a pack of those hairy Highlanders had rushed out to seize the horses."

"You mean Stuart's Highlanders?" the younger man asked. "No danger of that, my pretty. He's skulking around somewhere in the north."

"They do say," Miss Phipps answered, "that he is as handsome a man as a girl could hope to meet."

"Now, now!" The older man wagged a finger at her. "You will find Inverness full of English soldiers. And better a dragoon in the bed than a prince in the bush, eh?"

She shrieked, and with her free hand pushed his shoulder. My father said, from the corner where he sat huddled, "Please, madam! Please, sirs!" I knew that his indignation was not just on my behalf. He resented the manner in which they discussed the Prince.

The older man said, "Begging your and the young lady's pardon."

Miss Phipps looked at me, her rather fine eyes holding a strange blend of resentment and what appeared to be wistfulness. "Hoity-toity!" she said, and tossed her head. But after that all three of them, although they continued to drink, spoke less freely.

My father had not accepted the brandy offered by the Glasgow men, nor had he drunk from the bottle I knew he carried in the pocket of his greatcoat. I myself had bought the brandy.

I had gotten up that morning, after a night made almost sleepless by his coughing, and found my father awake, but still in his bed. He looked so ill—even more flushed than the night before, and with the skin drawn tight over his facial bones—that my heart contracted with terror. "We must stay here. You are unfit to travel."

"We have no money to stay here." He looked at his purse, lying on the washstand. "Go to an inn or grog shop. Get me some rum." When I stood silent, he said, "I know, Daughter. The one thing I never asked you to buy for our household was spirits. But believe me, it is medicine to me now. Without it I will not be able to rise from this bed. And I must."

In the ground floor hall I encountered Mrs. Ludlow. There were no inns nearby, she told me, and no grog shops open at that early hour. "I have no rum, but I can sell you brandy. There is only a little gone from the bottle. It will cost you three shillings."

I paid her, although I was sure she had overcharged me, and hurried back up the stairs, feeling weighted by far more than the bottle in my hand.

All that day, while the coach followed the road northward, sometimes across treeless moors, at other times beside rock-choked rivers foaming through narrow glens, I dozed and awoke, dozed and awoke. Thankfully I saw that my father sometimes slept too, despite the almost constant talk and laughter of our fellow passengers.

Around six o'clock we stopped at an inn, an establishment so rude that beyond its threshold I halted in disbelief. One room, apparently, served as parlor, taproom, kitchen, dining room, and bedroom of the couple who owned the place, for in a shallow recess at one side of the room stood a crudely made wooden bed. In the opposite wall were two doors which I assumed—correctly, as it turned out—led to separate sleeping quarters for men and women guests. In the center of the floor was the hearth, a circular pit whose smoke, or at least most of it, spiraled upward through a hole in the roof. Over the hearth a big cooking pot hung from a tripod.

Beside our own party, there were two other guests at the inn, a gaunt, middle-aged woman and her daughter, an equally gaunt spinster of about thirty-five. The older woman told us briefly that her man was dead, and that she and her daughter were traveling, mostly on foot, to Aberdeen, where they had kin. A guarded look in her eye made me wonder if her husband had died at Culloden, or at the hands of one of the search parties sent out to track down those who had managed to escape from the battlefield.

Despite the smoke stinging my nostrils and throat, I ate with good appetite the food served at a long table by our bald host—loaves of coarse bread, and rabbit stew which his carroty-haired wife measured out of the big pot into wooden bowls. When supper was finished, my father, who had eaten little, went to bed. So did the widow and her daughter and I, leaving only Miss Phipps and the Glasgow men at the table. In the women's quarters, I found that there was a bed large enough for two persons, and on the floor a number of pallets. As the youngest of the three, I of course took one of the pallets. Despite the lumpiness of the straw-filled mattress and the room's chill striking through the rough blanket, I soon fell asleep, and was only dimly aware, sometime in the night, of Miss

49

Phipps moving unsteadily past my pallet to one of her own.

In the morning I saw with reviving hope that my father seemed slightly improved. He ate at least a little breakfast and, once we had resumed our journey, sat more erect in his corner of the carriage. Miss Phipps and the Glasgow men, though, seemed lower in spirits. Perhaps there had been some quarrel among the three of them the night before. Perhaps yesterday's brandy did not sit well. Whatever the reason, they rode in silence broken only by an annoyed exclamation from Miss Phipps, or a muttered imprecation from the elder of the men, whenever a jounce of the coach flung them against each other. Shortly before noon, though, a bottle began to circulate among them, and soon their talk and laughter was almost as lively as during the day before.

We were traveling an upland moor by then. Every few minutes we saw evidence of the English revenge upon those who had fought for Charles Stuart at Culloden, or given refuge to those who survived the battle. We passed slaughtered cattle, grain fields burned to black stubble, and charred heaps which had once been farmhouses or herdsmen's huts. When Miss Phipps called it "a shocking sight," the younger of the Glasgow men retorted that the rebels were getting "their just deserts" for Falkirk, and for stealing English farmers' hogs and chickens while "Billy was chasing them north."

My father said nothing at all, but just grew more shrunken in his corner of the coach. I was not surprised when he reached inside his now stained and rumpled greatcoat, drew out a rum bottle he must have bought from the innkeeper that morning, and drank from it. Giggling, Miss Phipps parted her lips to speak. But perhaps the bleakness of my father's face touched her, because she made no comment.

I turned my head and looked out the window, aware of a hillside with thin mist now hiding, now revealing, brown rocks and green bracken, but not really seeing it. Soon this nightmare journey would be over. The coachman, we had learned at breakfast, hoped with a change of horses to reach Inverness soon after the long summer twilight ended. By day after tomorrow, conveyed there by some sort of vehicle, we would be at Bowain Castle. No need to fear that on Macduveen lands we would find burned huts and slaughtered cattle. Since the Macduveens had been, and no doubt still were, strong supporters of the Hanoverian monarchy, they would have been spared the attentions of the English search parties.

Again I wondered at my father's obvious dread of returning to the roof beneath which he had been born. Was it humiliation he feared? Perhaps, because he indeed would find it humiliating to return, ill and almost penniless, to kinfolk from whom he had parted, probably in anger, thirty years before. What was more, the Macduveens would be exultant over the defeat of the man he had crossed an ocean to serve. My heart ached for him, but at the same time I felt exasperated. In fact, ever since we had landed in Glasgow, I had felt a growing exasperation with male contentiousness in general, and Scotsmen's contentiousness in particular. My father himself had admitted that for centuries the Scots had fought, not only against the English, but with each other—Highlander against Lowlander, clan against clan, Catholic against Protestant, and various Protestant sects against other sects.

Near sunset we stopped at an inn to change horses and to eat a supper of cold mutton, turnips, and oaten cakes, baked on a griddle, which the innkeeper's wife called bannocks. We had resumed our journey, and were traveling along a hillside above a shallow valley, when the coach suddenly lurched to the right so violently that I was sure it would crash onto its side. Through Miss Phipps's scream and my own, I heard the crack of wood, and knew that the right rear wheel had broken. But the coach did not tip over. It remained at a steeply pitched angle, supported by some object at the roadside.

With difficulty the coachman forced the door open and helped us to the ground. I saw that the coach and its shattered wheel rested against a boulder. The coachman, a tall, dour-faced man, told us that a hare had run under the horses, causing them to rear. There would be no chance, he said, of repairing the wheel before darkness fell.

Fortunately the night was mild. While I stood at the roadside looking down a gentle slope to the dying gleam of a narrow river in the valley, the coachman and the Glasgow men ranged along the roadside, picking up pieces of wood and chunks of peat dropped from farmers' carts. Soon a fire was kindled. Its reddish light flickered over my father, lying huddled on the ground, silent except when coughs racked him, and over the coachman's somber face and the flushed and increasingly drunken faces of our three fellow passengers. At first indignant over the prospect of spending a night in the open, they now seemed to be enjoying it.

Their talk grew bawdier and bawdier. At last, when Miss Phipps and the younger man began a playful struggle over the handkerchief she had snatched from him and thrust into the bosom of her gown, the coachman rose and walked over to the iron-bound leather trunk attached to the rear of his disabled vehicle. He came back with a brown blanket folded over his arm. Standing with his back to the others, he said, "Take this, lass. Stay the night down by the river. Your father is asleep and has no need of you."

I was tired, and longed for solitude and silence. But still, to lie alone in a strange countryside, where wild beasts might pad silently toward me . . .

I said, "I have heard there are wolves in Scotland."

"Not many now. And in summer those few find game to feed them. They will not harm you. But what you witness here endangers your immortal soul."

I realized that here must be another sort of contentious man in this eternally quarrelsome land. Probably he belonged to the Covenanters, that most extreme of dissenting sects, who for a hundred years had not only warred against Popery, but found other Protestants insufficiently strict in their views.

I stood up and said in a low voice, "Spread the blanket over my father."

"Aye," the coachman said, after a moment, "he has more need of it, poor man." He covered the huddled figure on the ground with the blanket. My father stirred, but did not awaken. I don't think Miss Phipps and her companions were even aware that I slipped out of the circle of firelight.

There was no moon, but the stars were bright enough to guide me down the slope through the bracken. I paused once, but finding I could still hear talk and laughter, moved on. Finally I went around a copse—the trees looked like pines, although I could not be sure in that faint light—and chose a spot near the riverbank. Lying with my cloak wrapped closely around me, I pillowed my cheek on my hands. Somewhere nearby there was a waterfall, its sound as continuous as silence.

Longingly I thought of that castle in the western Highlands, where at least my father's fever-wasted body could find rest, no matter what the cost to his pride. With another sort of longing, a hopeless one, I thought of John Harwood, who perhaps by now had taken Charity Clayman or some other girl to the Harwood house as his bride. Then exhaustion overcame me, and I slept.

Perhaps some sound awoke me. Perhaps it was only the knowledge, penetrating through layers of sleep, that I was not alone. Whatever the reason, I came awake in the gray dawn and, my heart leaping with alarm, sat bolt upright.

There were five of them standing around me in an uneven circle. Bearded men in Highland dress, their long plaids tossed over their shoulders, their faces—ranging in age from youth to middle age—silent and intent. I said, trying to keep the quaver of fear out of my voice, "Who are you? What do you want?"

I heard the whispering sound of someone moving through the bracken. The circle parted, making way for another man, a tall one who appeared to be in his middle twenties. His fiery red hair was long and unkempt, his black coat rusty, his plaid kilt torn and muddy, and his legs and feet bare. And yet I think that I knew, even in those first few seconds, who he was.

His eyes—brown eyes, not the blue ones which often accompany that shade of hair—looked at me with surprise and amused sympathy. "You dolts, you have frightened her." He spoke with an accent I had never heard before. "Think what she must feel, waking to find herself surrounded by such wild-appearing men as yourselves." But there was no more real anger in his voice than in the smile that curved his mouth, a singularly handsome mouth with a full lower lip.

"Saving your pardon," the man on his left said with some asperity, "but 'tis you who is the dolt. There are people up on the road, no more than half a mile away, and no friends to us, judging by what I heard of their talk last night."

"Then go back into the copse. I will be with you soon. I wish to speak to this lady."

One of them muttered something that sounded like, "De'il take the lady." But they turned, waded through the bracken, and disappeared within the pinewood copse.

The red-haired man said, still smiling, "Are you of that coaching party?"

"Yes."

"I do not wonder that you chose to sleep here. Last night one of us came close enough to tell that they were far gone in their cups." He paused. "Are you English?"

"No, American."

"American!" From the copse came a soft whistle. He ignored it. "What part of America? Virginia, perhaps?"

"No, Long Island."

"The Long Island?"

He looked puzzled. I remembered how years ago my father had told me, to my astonished delight, that in Scotland Skye is called The Long Island.

"My Long Island is off the coast of America, south of Massachusetts Bay."

Another low whistle from the copse. He said, "Why is it that you have crossed the ocean, lady?"

I was silent for an indecisive moment. Then I said boldly, "It was my father's choice. He hoped to be of service to Charles Edward Stuart, as he was thirty years ago to James Stuart. But when we landed at Glasgow last Monday—"

My voice trailed off. He said wryly, "In Glasgow you learned that Charles had been no luckier than his father." Then, cheerful again: "But the game is not played out yet. Someday Charles may be able to welcome you to St. James. And a fine welcome he would give to a man who had crossed the ocean for the cause."

"I am afraid my father would not—" My throat began to close up, but I managed to say, "My father is very ill."

His smile vanished. "I am sorry to hear that."

"Once we reach Bowain Castle, perhaps he will get well."

"Bowain Castle?" He frowned. "The Macduveens? They are no friends of the Stuarts, you know."

"We know. But my father is not only ill. He is almost penniless. The Macduveens are our kin. We have no choice but to turn to them."

"What is your name, lady?"

"Elizabeth Logan."

Again that soft, urgent whistle from the copse. He said, "I wish you a safe arrival, Elizabeth Logan. And if it be of any comfort to you, know that in all my travels, and I have traveled much of late"—a wry smile twisted his mouth—"in all my travels, I have seen no face that pleased me more than yours. May it be your fortune, and may your father get well."

He turned and strode on muddy bare legs through the bracken. The copse swallowed him up.

I got to my feet and brushed bits of bracken from my cloak. Hopeful that the news would bring gladness to my father's eyes, I skirted the copse and hurried toward the distant road. After a while I heard the sound of metal against wood.

I found the coachman and a short, sturdy stranger, probably a man from some nearby croft, replacing the last of the wheel's shattered spokes with a new one. Miss Phipps and the Glasgow men stood in pale-faced, dispirited silence, watching the crofter force one end of the spoke into the hub. My father, huddled in his greatcoat, sat on the ground several yards away.

I sat down beside him. The face he turned to me was so flushed, so unnaturally bright of eye, that my heart contracted. No need to ask how he felt. But perhaps my news would be tonic to him. "Father," I whispered, "he is still alive, and free! I talked with him down by the river."

For a moment he appeared puzzled. Then his face cleared, and I knew he had understood. "Tell me! Did he appear in good spirits?"

"Remarkably so, for a man with a price on his head."

Answering my father's swift questions, I told him every detail of my encounter with the barefoot fugitive and his wild-looking entourage. "He speaks strangely, with an accent I never heard before."

"Of course, child. He speaks English as an Italian would. He grew up in Rome, remember."

A fit of coughing racked him. When he again turned his face to me, I saw that a certain vagueness had come into his eyes. "Tell me, lass, did ye find him bonnie?"

When I was a child, often he had amused me by speaking in the manner of the Highland common folk. Somehow it did not amuse me now. But all I said was, "Yes, Father. He is bonnie."

Seven

The cart, drawn by a shaggy little horse, drew us farther into the glen. It was so narrow that its turbulent stream almost touched the cart's creaking wheels as we moved along the dirt track, and so deep that its murky light might have been that of two hours past sunset instead of an hour before.

We were in the west now, that part of the Highlands which my father always had said was the most beautiful. But it was hard for me to appreciate the fragrance of ferns and the frothy white of a burn rushing down the hillside toward the narrow river. All my attention was centered upon my father. He lay on his side with knees bent in the small cart, his head pillowed upon my portmanteau. Through the creak of wheels and the sound of hurrying water, I could hear the rasp of his breath. I thought, with cold despair, "He is going to die."

As recently as two nights before in Inverness, I'd still felt hopeful. I had insisted that, even though the cost was staggering in that town overcrowded with soldiers with money to spend, he engage a private bedchamber at the inn. A night of undisturbed sleep, I had believed, might restore his flagging strength. In the morning, after a fairly restful night in a room I shared with only one other woman and her ten-year-old daughter, it was I who went to the innkeeper and asked how we might be transported to Bowain Castle. And it was I who, in the inn yard, agreed to pay one pound, plus his bill at the inn we would have to stop at on the way, to the crafty-faced carter who now sat up there on the narrow wooden seat. But all my efforts had served, not to dam my father's ebbing strength, but to drain most of what little was left in his purse.

We emerged into a wider valley where, in alternate sunlight and shadow, sheep grazed in the purple heather. From the valley floor the road rose in serpentine curves up the mountainside. We creaked slowly to the crest. And there my breathing, even my heartbeats, seemed to stop for a moment.

Below us lay a long, irregularly shaped loch, its cloud-shadowed waters a grayish blue. To the north and south of the loch rose wave upon wave of mountains, some a deep blue, and some, where the cloud cover was thinner, the purple of grapes. And to the west beyond the loch, where the sun shone, mountains rose in a ragged golden wave. I thought, "The mountains of Skye."

That was the moment when, despite our journey's hardships, despite those blackened fields and slaughtered cattle, despite even my despair over my father—that was the moment when I lost my heart to Scotland, never to recover it.

My father had grasped the side of the cart to pull himself to a sitting position. I asked, "Are those Skye's mountains?"

"They are." After a moment he added, "And that is Loch Ulain, where she drowned herself."

He meant Arabella, my great-aunt. How wretched indeed she must have been, to close her eyes willingly to all this wild beauty.

"Were you still in Scotland then, Father?"

"No, I had gone to London by then. But people talked of it, even there."

"Then are we close to Bowain Castle?"

After a moment he said, in a toneless voice, "It is not far."

"Lie down, Father. Rest."

Through light that brightened with sunset, we descended to the loch, followed its shore for a while, and then turned up another narrow glen. Twilight had begun when we emerged onto a vast, undulating moor. On rising ground near what I knew must be the moor's seaward edge, rose a stone tower, perhaps sixty feet high. Surely it must be the one of which my father had told me. The old, old tower, where from time to time, or so the legend said, a woman with a torch appeared behind that crenelated parapet.

And that other, much more massive structure at the moor's edge, perhaps three miles ahead of us, was surely Bowain Castle. I looked at my father. Although his eyes were closed, the tension in his thin face told me that he was not asleep. It also told me that there was no need to apprise him that his birthplace was near. He knew.

Ahead on the right rose an extensive wood of pines and

broad-leaved trees. Centuries ago, my father had told me, trees covered most of Scotland. But except for isolated stands they were gone now, felled to make ships in Aberdeen and Glasgow and London, leaving the moors to the heather and bracken and spiny gorse.

We were passing the wood now. The cartman half turned around on the seat. Was it just the cast in one eye that gave him that sly look? I did not think so. He said, pointing with his whip, "The lady could have saved herself a long walk."

"What lady?"

"The one as drowned herself." So he had been listening. "That's Bowain Wood. There's a pack of wolves in there that would have finished her off a lot quicker than the loch must have."

I look at him coldly, not speaking, until he turned back to his driving.

A few minutes later the cart creaked to a stop at the foot of a narrow road leading up to the castle. I saw now that it was of stone that probably was reddish, although it looked dark brown at this past-sunset hour. Above a solid foundation perhaps fifteen feet high, two rows of windows, gleaming dully in the twilight, stretched between the corner round towers. The carter turned on the seat, grinning, and said, "You are here."

I cried, "Aren't you taking us up to the castle?"

"It will cost you another shilling. That road is rough. I might break a wheel. And the horse is tired."

"The *horse* is tired! My father is ill, blast you! And you expect us to walk half a mile up a slope, carrying our—"

"Don't argue with him, Daughter." My father had low-

62

ered himself to the road, and now stood clutching the cart's side. "We have no shilling to spare. And besides, it is more fitting that we arrive on foot."

More fitting! Plainly the fever had clouded his mind. But I kept silent. Carrying the portmanteau, I got down to the road. The carter, looking disgruntled, took our small hand trunk from under the seat and handed it down to me. With a slap of the reins, he turned the cart and drove off. I said, through the dwindling creak of wheels, "I'll carry the hand trunk. And we will stop and rest every few yards."

As we started up the gentle slope, I saw for the first time that there was an archway near the southern end of the castle's high foundation. Beyond that archway we would find those who, no matter what the quarrels of thirty years before, would be bound by the ancient laws of kinship to shelter and care for my father. And perhaps, once he rested on a feather mattress and ate nourishing food, that shadow which seemed to hover almost visibly around him would lift, and he would be spared to me.

With a glad leap of my heart, I saw a coach, drawn by two sleek brown horses, emerge from the archway and move swiftly toward us. Evidently someone had glimpsed us from a window, and dispatched the coach to meet us.

My father had halted. As I too stopped and lowered the hand trunk to the ground, I was aware that he had taken off his beaver tricorn. The coach slowed, halted beside us. The passenger beyond the window was a plump, handsome woman of middle age, with a red-plumed black velvet hat set on her brown hair. Her round face had that placidity which can arise from either a spotless conscience

63

or a serene indifference to everything except one's own comfort. On the driver's box sat a sandy-haired man of forty-odd in worn green livery.

His small, good-natured eyes went from my father's face to mine, where they lingered for a moment with a faintly puzzled expression. Then he looked back at my father.

"Why, it's young Walter Logan! Although not so young now, are you, my friend? I'll swear the years have dealt more kindly with me, even allowing that I've lived half a dozen less of them. But I'd still know it is you, if only by that mickle scar on your forehead. I mind the day Jenny gave you that clout with a tankard's edge."

He paused. When my father said nothing, the coachman went on, with a chuckle, "You'd let the fire go out, and her with a suckling pig to roast. And so she picked up that tankard—"

"Kenneth, stop nattering." The woman in the plumed hat had leaned a little way out of the window. "Who are these people?"

The coachman turned on the high seat and looked down. "Walter Logan, milady. 'Twas before your time, but he was scullion here when I was stableboy. He ran off when I was nine or thereabouts. His father, old Walter, had been the castle shoemaker, and his mother was sempstress to Lady Macduveen. The first Lady Macduveen, I mean."

I accepted his words as true. But I accepted them only as one, in the numbing grip of a nightmare, accepts as true the fact that the turning of a familiar head has revealed the grotesque face of an utter stranger.

64

The woman I realized must be Lady Macduveen looked at me. "Are you his daughter?"

I nodded, unable to speak.

"Begging your pardon, milady, but I take it that the Lady Macduveen I knew is dead." My father's labored voice was dull, humble, and shorn of all its cultivated modulations. If he had not been standing right beside me, hat in his hands, shoulders hunched beneath his greatcoat, I would not have believed it was he who spoke.

"Oh, yes. She died twenty-seven years ago."

"And Sir James?"

"He has been dead for five years. My son, Sir Donald, is the present laird." She paused, a shade of concern in her rather prominent brown eyes as my father bent over in a coughing fit. Finally she said, "But my good man, you are ill!" Alarm crossed her face. "You are not carrying plague, are you?"

I found I could speak. "It is not plague. He has a congestion of the lungs. He has had it for weeks."

She frowned slightly, as if she found something in my manner not to her liking. Then her brow cleared. "You may go up to the castle. Someone will give your father a place to lie down until he is better. And tell them in the kitchen that you are to be given employment. Drive on, Kenneth."

The smile she gave us, as the coach began to move, seemed to hold a sense of her own graciousness. But that she should leave us to struggle up the slope, and still think herself generous, did not surprise me. It was just part of the bleak reality, hidden until now, that the coachman's words had revealed.

I grasped my father's arm. "Sit down." When he was seated on the hand trunk, his hat once more shadowing his face, I stood looking down at him. Even today I turn sick with shame at memory of the rage which shook me. "Now tell me," I said. *"Tell* me. And no more lies."

Eight

He did not speak, but just raised his eyes to my face, the hopelessly guilty eyes of a whipped dog. My handsome father, whose jaunty elegance had always been my delight. My anger disappeared under a flood of sorrowful tenderness. Dropping to the ground, I laid my hand on his bony fevered one. "Please. I must know now, while we are still alone. Why did you lie?"

His voice sounded very tired, but strangely calm, as if the abandonment of deception brought him a kind of peace. "I lied because I so wanted to be a gentleman. I always wanted that, even as a small boy. You see, my mother could read. She learned it from her father, a crofter who had wanted to be a priest before priesthood became too dangerous, and when I was six, she began to teach me. That alone made me feel I was set apart from the other servants."

He stopped speaking. I said, "Was anything of what you told me true? Did you really fight in the 1715 Rising?"

"I did. Both my parents were dead then. I ran away and

fought for James Stuart at the Battle of Preston, and after the battle was lost, I went to London."

He stopped speaking. Steeling myself to ask the question, I said, "And your scar?"

"I got it as Kenneth said, when I was fourteen." The thickening of his voice told me that he was reliving the shame and rage of that long-ago moment. In my mind's eye I saw the heavy tankard raised in the hand of a faceless person named Jenny—cook? scullery maid?—and saw its edge bite deep into the young boy's forehead.

"And in London, Father?"

"I became an actor at the Drury Lane." There was a faint note of pride in his labored voice. "I played Sheridan, and Congreve."

"Is that how you learned to dress and speak like—like—"

"No, it was chiefly a woman I had to thank for that. But I can not talk of it. It is not a story for the ears of an innocent girl, especially one's own daughter."

"Innocent!" Some of my anger returned. "That is an excuse men use when they want to keep us ignorant of things we should know. And you have kept me ignorant far too long."

He told me, then. The woman had been a rich merchant's widow, more than twice my father's age, and with grown children. She had come to the theater one evening. The next day she had sent a note to him in care of the theater manager. The final result was that he took up residence in her house, and lived there for seven years.

She must have regarded him as a son as well as a lover, for she provided him with tutors in Greek, Latin, and mathematics, and later secured his entrance to Oxford.

68

When she contracted what she correctly guessed to be a fatal illness, she gave him a thousand pounds. After her death, he emigrated to Southampton, purchased his property on Job's Lane, married my mother, and set himself up as tutor to the sons of prosperous and ambitious fathers.

"There seemed little chance of anyone ever learning the truth about me. And so there seemed no harm in—representing myself as I did."

No harm, except that he had falsified his whole life. Why had he done it? Was it to try to deny what he saw each time he looked in the mirror? That scar, like a shameful brand, reminding him that once he had been a potboy at the mercy of a brutal fellow servant?

"And by the time you were three, I was glad of the lies. Your face was taking shape even then, and you had that proud, spirited way of carrying your head. I felt you had a right to think yourself of gentle blood."

I wanted to say, "But I did not care about that!" When he had talked of Scotland, what had enchanted me had been the thought of Castle Bowain and the western Highlands, not the titled people I had believed to be my kinfolk. Aside from being Walter Logan's daughter, the only distinction I had ever aspired to was to be John Harwood's wife.

John. As I sat here in this strange and cruel and beautiful land, with the moor stretching around me in the deepening dark, it seemed to me that John and the tree-shadowed streets of Southampton were not merely an ocean away, but on another planet.

I said, "But why didn't you tell me the truth in Boston, or while we were on the ship?"

"Because I hoped that in a way I could make the lie come true. They say that the Prince is generous to his friends. I hoped that, by attaching myself to his cause . . ."

I thought of Charles Edward, that handsome scarecrow, standing with bare, scratched legs knee-deep in bracken. That fugitive with no lands or titles to bestow, with nothing, in fact, but the loyalty of such rough-looking friends as those who had waited in the copse, and his own undaunted cheerfulness.

I said, "Do you think you can go on now? It is almost dark."

He nodded. I helped him to his feet and handed him the portmanteau. He stood there, swaying, while I picked up the hand trunk. With him leaning against me, we started up the slope.

Nine

The old man named Angus had brought a candle stub into the shed. Its light wavered over the rotting floor, the broken stalls where cattle once must have stood, and over the heap of straw where my father lay, his eyes narrowed to slits through which the whites showed. He no longer coughed, but drew each breath with a labored, rasping sound that filled me with despair.

He had managed to stay on his feet until we had moved through the archway and along a vaulted tunnel into the courtyard. Dimly I was aware of a rear archway, above which a torch burned, and of a row of wooden shacks stretching along the high stone wall to my left, and of one-story buildings along the wall opposite. The first of those stone buildings, apparently, was the castle kitchen, for flickering firelight fell through its wide doorway onto the cobblestones. We had taken only a step or so toward that doorway when my father collapsed into a heap beside me.

With a cry, I knelt on the cobblestones. As I loosened the stained and wrinkled stock knotted around his throat, I was aware of approaching footsteps. I looked up to see a white-bearded man standing over us, and a tall girl of about my own age whose long dark hair sprang from low on her forehead, and an even taller woman of late middle age. "Please," I said, "could you—"

"Who are you?" the woman asked. Her small eyes, which appeared gray in this uncertain light, were staring at my upturned face with an antagonism which seemed as strong as it was inexplicable.

"My father's name is Walter Logan," I said swiftly. "Mine is Elizabeth. Please help me to—"

"Walter Logan!" Grunting with effort, she leaned over and plucked the hat from his head. "So it is," she said, straightening. She gave a brief laugh, and dropped his hat to the cobblestones. "Ran away to help your precious Papist, didn't you, young Walter? And now you are back. What for? To help his son play hide-and-seek with the English?"

I said, trying to control my fury, "Lady Macduveen told us we could find shelter here."

She looked at me with such enmity that for a moment I thought she was going to turn her back on us. Then she said, "You, Mag. Help Angus get him into the old cowshed. And then come back to the kitchen. You mind? Her ladyship is bringing two more guests for supper, as if it wasn't enough with Clarence MacElvin and his wife here. So don't you dawdle, hear?"

The girl's voice was sullen. "Aye, Jenny."

Carrying the hand trunk and the portmanteau, I followed the old man and the girl as they half dragged, half carried my father across the cobblestones. Inside the shed, its doorway so low that the old man and the girl had to stoop, they lowered him to a pile of straw in one corner.

When they had gone, I sat on the floor, listening to the labored breath, my eyes fixed on the face that was only a pale blur in the deepening darkness.

After a while Angus had returned. In one hand he carried the lighted stub of a candle set in an earthenware dish, and in the other a stone jug with a pewter cup inverted over its mouth. He set the candle on a stall rail, and the jug on the dirt floor beside me. "I've brought you water, lass." Then, looking down at my father: "He looks verra sair, poor man."

That was one of the old Scottish expressions with which my father used to amuse me. For a moment my throat closed up. Then I said, "Yes, I fear he is."

" 'Twere better he sleeps now. But when he wakes, ask Jenny for a drop of broth."

Jenny, the woman who had scarred a young boy for life. A powerful-looking woman even now, she must have been a veritable Amazon thirty years before. "Did you know my father?"

"No, Jenny says he was potboy here, but that was before my time. Lady Macduveen brought me here as chief hosteler. The second Lady Macduveen, that is." He paused. "If you have need of me, the stables are back of the courtyard. You'll find me there."

He left me then. I do not know how long I sat there. Through my father's labored breathing I now and then heard other sounds. Shouts of laughter and young masculine voices singing came from somewhere above, probably from the castle windows overlooking the courtyard. Metal pots banged in the kitchen, and once I heard Jenny upbraiding someone, probably the girl Mag. Then, when the candle had almost burned down into its pool of grease, I heard a carriage stop in the entrance tunnel. There had been an open door there, I recalled, with a flight of stairs leading upward. I heard several voices, including Lady Macduveen's. Then the empty coach, with the coachman Kenneth on the box, rolled across the cobblestones toward the courtyard's rear archway.

Perhaps it was the sound that woke my father. "Bess?" I leaned over him. "How do you feel?"

He did not answer. His gaze was moving over the rough beams overhead, and the stall's rotting rails. "In the morning," I lied, "you are to have a room with a real bed. Wouldn't you like some broth now?" He shook his head. "Please, Father!"

"Very well." Then, as I started to rise, he laid thin fingers on my wrist. "Some of what you always believed was true. I am sure of it. You are my surety."

I said, with despair, "Yes, Father." He was slipping from me fast now. His mind was clouded, and the fingers lying on my wrist were no longer fevered, but very cold. "I'll get you the broth."

I hurried across the cobblestones. In the shadowy kitchen Jenny sat on a stool beside the still-flickering embers in the huge fireplace. A half-plucked goose, long neck dangling, lay across her lap. I said, "May I take my father some broth?"

She looked at me, coldly silent. Then, swiveling around on the stool, she faced a doorway in the far corner of the room. I heard footsteps climbing stone stairs. The girl Mag, grasping an uncorked wine bottle in each hand, entered the room. "You are not to take the wine up," Jenny said. Then, as angry protest flared in the girl's face: "Oh, I know. You were hoping to flaunt yourself before Sir Donald. As if he'd look at a great, gawky, ill-shaken-up creature like you."

The words were unjust. Except for that too-low forehead, Mag was handsome enough in her tall, large-boned fashion. Jenny nodded toward me. "This one will take the wine up."

I cried, "But my father—"

"Her ladyship sent down word that you are to work for your keep. But first, take off your cloak."

Trembling with anger, I took off my cloak, folded it onto one of the several stools standing before the fireplace, and grasped the bottles Mag sullenly held out to me. "Where shall I take them?"

"Up the stairs." She nodded toward an archway in the opposite corner of the kitchen from the cellar entrance.

"To which floor?"

"The first. The top one is used for storage, although in the old days, when Sir James and his first wife were alive, and there were lots of servants . . . But never mind that. Don't dawdle by the dining hall. Sir Donald and his friends are there. Just keep on until you reach the last door."

As if I would dawdle anywhere, I thought with helpless fury, when my father's life was slipping away minute by minute. I hurried to the archway in the corner and found myself at the foot of narrow stairs spiraling upward through the castle's northern round tower. From somewhere above came a flickering, reddish glow. I rounded the first of the spirals and saw, set in deep embrasures in the curving wall, a row of arrow slits. Above them a torch burned in an iron socket. I followed the spiral upward a few more feet, and then stepped through an open doorway into a wide corridor, dimly illuminated by tapers set in widely spaced wall sconces. From a doorway up ahead came boisterous male laughter.

I hurried forward, head down, gaze fixed on the narrow strip of carpet, so worn that I could not discern its pattern. That was why I did not see, until I was only a step away from him, that a man lounged against one side of the open doorway. In the corridor near his feet sat a rough-coated deerhound, almost as large as a pony.

The man reached out and caught my arm. "Well! What have we here?"

As I tried to pull away, I looked over his shoulder and caught a brief impression of drink-flushed young men gathered around a long table, and of a stone wall hung with crossed pistols and swords, glinting in the candle-light. One of the young men, a grin on his face, was moving toward the doorway. Still grasping my arm with one hand, my captor reached out and closed the door.

"Now," he said, "who are you? A new serving wench?" His gaze was sweeping my brown linsey dress. "Not by the look of you."

My voice shook. "Let go of me!"

"Now, now, girl. Do you know who I am? I am Donald Macduveen."

So this was the young laird. He was plump, like his mother, and perhaps two inches taller than I, with a blond peruke set slightly askew, revealing the limp brown hair underneath. I guessed his age to be twenty-three or -four, although the spoiled set of his full mouth made him look younger than that, and the dissipated fullness under his brown eyes much older.

"Let me go," I said. "And don't make me drop this

wine. Your—her ladyship has sent for them."

"Then you are a serving wench." His tone was sneering, but perhaps my mention of his mother had daunted him a little, because he released my arm. I hurried on down the hall and stopped at a partially open door at its end. From beyond it came a babble of voices. Still grasping the bottles, I knocked with the knuckles of my right hand, but evidently talk and laughter covered the sound, because no one bade me enter. With my shoulder I pushed the door farther open and took a few tentative steps into the room.

I had an impression of candlelight and dying firelight, of a table littered with silver drinking vessels and with china plates which bore the remnants of a supper. Around a bird cage which hung between two of the room's tall windows, a half dozen or more middle-aged, richly dressed men and women were gathered. Fleetingly I realized that those windows, like the ones in the dining hall, must overlook the courtyard. Then I saw Lady Macduveen seated beside the dying fire. On her lap was some sort of needlework, perhaps a square of tapestry, in its wooden frame. Beside her stood a tall woman of forty-odd, with elaborately dressed dark hair and a proud, coldly handsome face. "I think, Mrs. MacElvin, that I will work a rose into this corner . . ." Then, suddenly aware of my presence: "Yes?"

"I have brought some wine, your ladyship."

Perhaps my strange accent had caught the attention of the group around the bird cage. I was aware of turning heads and the clatter of someone's silver wine cup falling to the floor.

"Put it on the table." I placed the bottles on the wine-stained cloth and turned away. "Wait," Lady Macduveen said. "Did you tell me your name?"

I turned back. "It is Elizabeth Logan."

Perhaps I should not have given my full name. Or perhaps again something in my manner struck her as unsuitable, because the shadow of a frown touched her placid brow. "Here you will be called Betty. Leave us now, Betty."

At least, I thought, moving toward the door, she would not be calling me Bess. Only my father had ever called me that.

I found the corridor empty. The sounds of revelry came muted now from behind the dining hall's closed door. I hurried past it. Only three more doors, one of them open, between me and the round tower stairs. Soon I would be spooning broth into my father's mouth.

Sudden movement in the darkness just beyond that open door. An arm encircled me, pinning my arms to my side. A hand covered my mouth, its finger biting into my cheeks. I caught a glimpse of Donald Macduveen's round face. His plump upper lip was lifted at the corners in what was both a sneer and a smile. Then he had dragged me into the darkened room.

I fought, writhing in his grasp and kicking at his fat legs. I worked my lips apart far enough to sink my teeth into his palm. Cursing, he released me momentarily. I lunged toward the doorway, only to feel his hand grasp the shoulder of my dress. I heard a ripping sound, and felt his other arm close around me.

Someone's tall body blocked out the light from the doorway. Someone's hand grasped the collar of Donald Macduveen's coat and jerked him into the corridor. I found myself leaning against the door jamb, looking daz-edly at the two men—one young and plump and scarlet-faced with rage, the other perhaps ten years older than my father, a tall man with a saturnine face and no peruke on a dark head still untouched with gray.

"You puppy," the tall man said. "You worthless, wenching puppy."

Donald said thickly, "It's no concern of yours, Clarence MacElvin."

Clarence MacElvin, evidently the husband of that hand-some woman who had stood looking down at her hostess's needlework. And, long ago, another woman's husband? Yes, surely my father had told me that the beautiful and tragic Arabella had been the bride of a Clarence MacElvin.

"You are only a guest here," Donald was saying. "And after a fortnight you've worn out your welcome. I'm mas-ter here, and I tell you that to your face."

"Master?" Clarence MacElvin's voice was cold. "At the expense of whose purse? Who was it who, four years ago, kept this roof from being sold over your worthless head?"

After a moment Donald muttered, "It was your brother more than you." Then, as if aware of the feebleness of his response, he turned and hurried away. The door of the dining hall closed behind him.

Clarence MacElvin's dark gaze fastened on my face. "Who are you?" Then, as I opened my mouth to speak: "I heard you tell your name. How is it you are here?"

I owed him an answer. Agonizing as I found the delay, I owed him that. "My father was a servant here as a boy, and so were both his parents. He is very ill now, and with no money. We had no other place to go."

He nodded, no expression in his dark, high cheekboned

79

face, and walked away toward the end of the hall. I hurried down to the shadowy kitchen. Jenny must have finished plucking the goose and placed it in the larder, because now she stood stirring the contents of a big iron kettle that hung from a tripod above the hearth's glowing embers. On the floor in the far corner of the room, on a bed that consisted of a heavy layer of straw, Mag lay beneath a blanket. She was not asleep. I could see the dull gleam of her eyes, watching me over her blanketed shoulder.

Thankfully, I saw that an empty wooden bowl and a wooden spoon now rested on one of the fireside stools. "May I have the broth?"

Her gaze, fixed on my shoulder, reminded me of my ripped dress. She said, "Sir Donald's work, I'll warrant. Didn't I tell you to stay away from the dining hall?"

What use to explain what had happened? "If the broth—"

"In the morning you can put on a dress of Mag's. You've nothing fit for a kitchen wench, if what you have on is a sample. And you'll sleep over there with Mag. I'll put down another blanket."

Had she no intention of giving me the broth? Abandoning my efforts at self-control, I cried, "Why do you hate me so? Why do you hate my father?"

She turned toward me, arms akimbo. "Because his mother followed the Antichrist!" I realized that she must mean the Pope. "Oh, she did not say so. But we all knew she wore a crucifix stuffed down inside her shift. And many a time I heard her praying to the saints. The saints! Heathen idols is more like it, what with those statues of them in the Papist churches. Yes, and in the Anglican

churches too. A Christian needs no saints to stand between him and God, and no priests or bishops, either."

She paused for breath, and then went on, "I'll warrant
Walter Logan is a Papist. It was a poison he must have
drawn in with his mother's milk. And like as not you are a
idolater too."

I might have answered that in Southampton I had listened each Sunday to a minister whose creed was probably no less stern than her own, and that my father, if he
seldom heard the minister's sermons, always contributed
to his salary. But I would not demean my father and
myself to that extent. No, not even for the broth.

But apparently she had vented her spleen, because she
picked up the wooden bowl, ladled broth into it, and held
it out to me. With muttered thanks I took it, picked up my
folded cloak from the stool, and left her. As I crossed the
cobblestones, the steam from the broth reminded me that
I had eaten nothing since that morning. And yet I felt no
hunger.

Light wavered beyond the shed's doorway. Someone,
most probably Angus, had brought a fresh candle. I entered the shed, looked down at my father, and saw instantly that he too would not want the broth. Each breath
was a rattle in his chest. His eyes were glazed, and the
shape of every bone was discernible beneath the skin of his
face. I placed the bowl on a stall rail, and dropped to my
knees beside him.

He said, "Get me a priest."

So she had been right, that fanatic who presided over
the castle kitchen. My thoughts scattered wildly. How
could I find a priest in this strange, dark countryside
stretching away from this ancient stone pile? Whom could

I even ask about a priest, here in this household where the gentry adhered to the Church of England, and where all the servants, perhaps, shared Jenny's hatred of Catholics? "Father—"

He drew a rattling breath. "I'm dying, Bess. Get me a priest."

Old Angus. He had been kind, and was therefore my only hope. I got to my feet and started out of the shed, so hurriedly that I tripped over the doorsill. It was only by grasping the door frame that I saved myself from pitching to the cobblestones. I stood there for a moment to catch my breath. Across the courtyard, I saw now, Jenny had closed the kitchen door for the night.

A flash and an explosive sound from behind one of those slits in the north tower. Simultaneously, it seemed to me, something struck the side of the shed a foot or so from where I stood, and then fell with a metallic clatter to the cobblestones.

I stood rooted with incredulity. Had someone fired a pistol ball at me? I thought of Donald Macduveen's anger-flushed face. But surely he was not that angry, nor that vicious. Perhaps one of his drunken friends, who were still shouting and singing up there behind those lighted windows, had taken one of those pistols down from the wall, gone to the north tower, and fired at random into the courtyard. Still, if the ball had landed a foot or so to the left . . .

But it had not, and I had no time to waste more thought on it. I hurried across the courtyard and through the rear archway.

Ten

Through the wide door of a wooden building directly ahead, I could see Angus kneeling beside the coach's right rear wheel, wiping mud from its spokes with what looked like part of an old shirt. I stepped through the doorway into air redolent of hay and dung and leather.

"Angus." Dimly I was aware of the sound of tethered horses moving restless hooves somewhere in the shadowy reaches to my right.

He turned his head and then got laboriously to his feet. Fleetingly I noticed that his eyes were blue and strangely young-looking in his seamed face. "My father is dying." My throat felt so swollen that I had to force the words out. "He wants a priest."

Pity and dismay came into the blue eyes. "Child—"

"Isn't there a priest somewhere near?"

After a moment he said, in a low voice, "There is Mr. Jameson in Garlaig. If I saddle Bluebell right now, happen I could fetch him here in time he could get back home before daylight."

"He does not want a minister!" I became aware I was

twisting my hands together. "He asks for a priest."

His voice sank even lower. "Mr. Jameson is a priest. But where Macduveens and MacElvins are lairds, it has long been wise for a priest to call himself mister."

My agonized doubt must have shown in my face, because he said, "He is a priest, lass, even though he wears no vestments and has no parish. Catholics believe that once a man is ordained of God, he has the priestly power until he dies. Even though I am no Papist, I know that much about their faith. Now go back to your father, child."

I turned away.

For an unmeasured interval I sat beside my father in the shed. When I had told him that a priest would be with him soon, a look of profound gratitude had come into his eyes. But he had not spoken then, or since. I felt that he was concentrating all the strength that remained to him on staying alive until the priest's arrival. Eyes fixed on his gray face, I too tried to will that those painful breaths would not cease until I heard the priest's footsteps.

Once, despite my concentration on the labored rise and fall of his chest, another thought intruded. That object which had struck the side of the shed and then fallen to the cobblestones. Was it still there? I went outside. No light shone from the dining hall windows now, but the torch above the courtyard's rear archway still sent a wavering light over the cobblestones. I knelt, and with flattened palms felt all around the area where the pistol ball had probably fallen. It was not there. Had it ever been there? Had I, in my distraught state, imagined the sharp explosion of a pistol and the impact of an iron ball against the shed's side? Or had someone, while I talked to Angus in the stable, come down to the courtyard and retrieved the ball? I got to my feet and went back to my father.

I had been sitting beside him perhaps ten minutes, in silence broken only by that labored breathing, when Angus and a plump, mild-faced man, wearing brown homespun breeches and coat, entered the shed. Angus said, "I have brought Mr. Jameson." He looked down at my father and then said to me, "Come, child. 'Tis best to leave them alone."

Outside the shed Angus and I moved a few yards away over the cobblestones and then halted. He said gently, "From the look of your father, a coffin will be needed soon. I will ask Kenneth to help. He is a good lad. And his nephew will help too. Call me when you have need of me." He moved toward the rear archway.

I looked up at the black sky. Strange that there was no dawn glimmer. It seemed to me that many hours had passed since, with my father leaning against me, I had entered this courtyard.

Footsteps. I turned to see Mr. Jameson's plump figure moving toward me. He touched my shoulder. "His heart and mind are at ease now, my child. Go to him."

I found my father conscious. He smiled at me, and then closed his eyes. Even though he still breathed with that labored, rattling sound, his face was peaceful. I do not know how much longer I sat there. I only knew that suddenly I became aware that his breath had ceased.

I placed my ear to his chest. No sound. I kissed his forehead and then looked down at the wasted, peaceful face. I knew that soon grief and loneliness would tear at me. But now all that I felt was a vast emptiness. I rose and left the shed.

Outside the courtyard's rear archway I paused. From somewhere up the line of low outbuildings came the sound of hammering. Angus and Kenneth, constructing my father's coffin. Moving farther away from the courtyard wall, I looked toward the invisible horizon. Still no sign of dawn's approach.

But a star, low in the sky, was shining through the clouds. No, not a star. Some sort of man-made light. As I strained my eyes through the darkness, it seemed to me that I could make out the shape of that many-centuries-old round tower, a deeper black against the black sky. Was that lady of the legend upon the parapet tonight? No, it was not wavering torchlight I saw, but rather a steadier, paler gleam, like that of a lantern. And did it shine from the parapet, or through some narrow window in the tower itself? I could not tell. Even as I looked at it, it disappeared.

I heard footsteps, and saw Angus's tall, lean shape moving toward me. When he was still a few feet away, he halted and asked, "Is he gone, then?"

Still aware of nothing but emptiness, I said, "Yes."

After a moment's silence he said, "Lass, he cannot be buried in consecrated ground. There is not a Catholic graveyard in many miles. True, there is the graveyard beside the kirk in Garlaig, but I fear that your father, a stranger in this place—"

"It does not matter." Remembering the peace of his face, I felt that his soul would not care where his body rested.

"Best that you not go back to the shed. Leave matters to Kenneth and me. There is an empty stall in the stable. The straw is clean. Will you rest there until Kenneth and

I have finished?"

"Yes," I said, and turned away.

Through the first gray light we moved along the faint
path which led across the moor's spiny gorse and purple
heather. Kenneth and Angus walked ahead of me, carrying the roughly made coffin by its rope handles. Far ahead
of us and to the left, the ancient round tower rose on its
low promontory, its stones dark red in the dawn light.

We had walked the better part of an hour when the path
began to slant upward toward a grove of juniper and pine.
We moved through the trees and into a grassy open space
beyond. A sandy-haired young boy I realized must be Kenneth's nephew stood there, leaning on a shovel beside the
open grave. Beyond him I could see a line of gorse bushes.
I knew they must mask the edge of a headland overlooking
the sea, because I could hear the break and withdrawing
seethe of each separate wave.

When the coffin had been lowered, the two men and the
boy stepped back. I moved to the graveside and stood
looking down at the hastily made wooden box which held,
not my father, but the exhausted body which he had at
last been able to escape. I thanked God for that peaceful
look on my father's face, and prayed that his soul was
indeed at rest.

I turned away then and moved through the screen of
gorse. Yes, this was headland, sloping away to a rocky
beach about a hundred and fifty feet below. From behind a
curtain of offshore mist, gray waves rolled to break foaming on the shore. From behind me, almost drowned out by
the waves, came the scraping sound of the shovel.

When the scraping ceased, I turned and moved back

through the gorse bushes. Angus and Kenneth and the boy stood beside the mounded grave. For the first time I noticed that beyond them, near the pines and juniper, there was another low mound, blanketed with coarse grass. Kenneth looked at me, his good-natured little eyes holding a sympathy he evidently did not know how to put into words. Then he nodded and, with his nephew beside him, turned and disappeared through the trees.

I said into the silence. "Whose grave is that?"

"A lady's. She was sister to the old laird, Sir James Macduveen. She died long ago, several years before I came here with the second Lady Macduveen."

"Was she Arabella? The one who drowned herself only a few months after she married Clarence MacElvin?"

"Yes. Some say she did it because it was Clarence's younger brother that she loved. I do not know, since it was before my time here. But anyway, the poor lady could not be buried in consecrated ground, not when she had taken her own life. I hear there were those who said she should be buried at the crossroads, with a stake driven through her heart. But neither the Macduveens or the MacElvins would stand for that, so she was buried here."

I walked over to the unmarked grave of Arabella Macduveen MacElvin. Arabella who, in my father's lie about his origins, had been his aunt, and therefore my great-aunt. Had he confessed that lie, among his other sins and follies, to the priest? Whether he had or not, he must have felt shriven of it, or he would not have died with that look on his face.

Angus had walked over to stand beside me. Reaching inside his shirt, he brought out my father's purse. "This is yours now."

Opening it, I spilled a few coins into my hand, and saw that they added up to two shillings, six pence. As my left hand funneled them back into the leather pouch, he asked, "What will you do now?"

"What can I do, except work for my keep?"

Those strangely young eyes studied my face. "I give you sympathy, lass, but no pity. You do not have need of it. You have a brave heart and a pleasing face. That will serve you in place of silver in your purse."

Who else had said something like that to me? Oh, yes, Charles Edward, standing tattered and cheerful in the bracken.

"Will you come back with me now, child?"

Back to the castle and placidly selfish Lady Macduveen and her loose-lipped son. Back to the cavernous kitchen and fanatical Jenny and sullen-faced Mag. At the very thought I felt tired, so tired that I feared I would sway on my feet.

"Leave me here. I must sleep for a little while."

"Aye, that would be best. Nothing will harm you here."

His tall form disappeared through the trees. I walked back toward my father's grave and lay down a few feet from it, my cloak wrapped tightly around me.

Somewhere among the trees a bird began to sing. It must have been a thrush, because its soft, sweet warble reminded me of the tawny-breasted bluebirds who came to eastern Long Island each spring to build their nests in hollow trees. That gentle sound was the last I heard before exhaustion overcame me and I slept.

Eleven

One afternoon almost three months later I stood at the parapet of the castle's northern tower, gazing across the strait's blue waters toward the grape-purple mountains of Skye. Sun fell warm on my face and my forearms. I had rolled to the elbow the much-too-long sleeves of the faded blue homespun dress which Mag, at Jenny's order, had sullenly bestowed upon me. And as I stood there, breathing air that smelled of sea and sun-warmed heather, I was happy.

Most would say I had little reason to be. I was still utterly alone in the world. For my keep, and a promised two pounds a year, I worked hard from first light until after Gerald, the aged footman Lady Macduveen had brought to the castle years before, carried the gentry's dinner dishes down to the kitchen. When Lady Macduveen or Sir Donald had guests staying with them, as they frequently did, I worked even longer hours, helping the two elderly chambermaids sweep and dust and change bed linen. What was more, I had no real reason to hope that my situation would improve.

But when one is eighteen, it is almost impossible not to hope. At eighteen, when the blood runs warm and swift through the veins, often it is happiness just to be alive. Too, working under Jenny's supervision had proved less galling than I had feared. In my first raw grief I had even welcomed familiar tasks like candlemaking and roasting fowl on the spit. And I had welcomed the necessity to learn new skills, such as baking bannocks on a griddle. During those first few days, as I carried water from the courtyard well or mixed batter for bannocks, I sometimes saw reluctant approval in Jenny's small gray eyes.

On the third morning, as she and Mag and I sat on the fireplace stools plucking grouse and dropping the feathers into a wooden tub, Jenny said, "You are a puny-appearing lass. But I vow you seem almost as strong as this great gawk Mag here, and much more quick." Seeing the sullen fury in Mag's dark eyes. I wished that Jenny had saved her grudging praise until she and I were alone.

It was daily association with Mag that I found hardest to bear—harder than the long hours of toil, and Jenny's often rough tongue, and the sneering look Donald Macduveen gave me on those rare occasions when I met him in the castle corridor. For most of my first week here I reluctantly had gone to bed beside Mag in that straw-strewn corner of the kitchen. Then one night I awoke with a start. On her own blanket, not two feet from mine, Mag sat staring down at me. Moonlight coming through the kitchen's one window shone on her face, broad and pale in its frame of coarse black hair, and gave her dark eyes a cold gleam. My stomach knotted with distaste and something like fear. How long had she sat there, eyes fastened on my sleeping face?

I kept my voice low, so as not to waken Jenny, over there on her pallet beside the banked fire. "What are you doing?"

Her lips curved in a slow smile. "Watching you. What is the harm in that?"

My anger stirred. Why was she so hostile? Because I was a stranger? Because, the first night I spent in this kitchen, I had betrayed my reluctance to sleep in my shift, as she and Jenny did? Or was it because it had been I, rather than she, who had received, and violently rejected, the young laird's amorous attentions?

I said sharply, "Well, stop it. If you don't, in the morning I'll tell Jenny."

She waited several seconds, apparently to convey that she was not daunted by my threat, and then lay down. The next day, giving no reason, I asked Jenny if there was someplace else I could sleep.

"So your ladyship wants her own chamber, does she? Maybe you want to sleep upstairs with the gentry."

"I was hoping I might take one of the huts."

The courtyard huts, I had learned, dated from the days when Bowain Castle had at times had to withstand enemy attack. The wooden huts along one wall had housed cattle hastily driven in from the moors, and pigs and chicken and geese. The stone building along the opposite wall had included, not just the kitchen, but a stable for horses, a carpenter shop, and a smithy.

Jenny shrugged. "If you will clean it out, you can use the stone hut at the far end. Lady Macduveen and Sir Donald get their shoes from Glasgow now. But time was, in Sir James's day, that old Walter Logan made shoes for the gentry and the servants too."

Old Walter Logan, my grandfather.

"Of course, there's a hole in the roof. You'll have to put your pallet in one corner, out of the rain. And come winter, you'll be glad enough to sleep in here with Mag and me, I'll warrant."

That afternoon when I was free from the kitchen for a few hours, I cleaned the cobbler's hut of its dirt and cobwebs and its nests, made of plant fibers and bits of paper and cloth, in which many generations of field mice must have nurtured their young. In one corner, well away from the gaping hole in the roof, I spread the clean straw Angus had brought from the stable, and placed my two blankets upon it.

That night, when my after-supper chores were finished, I left the kitchen and walked toward the cobbler's hut. Then, so that I could anticipate for a while longer the moment when I would enter the lovely solitude of my new home, I moved through the courtyard's rear archway. Beyond the last of the line of outbuildings, I stopped at the moor's edge and looked up at the star-brilliant sky. I was about to turn back when I saw a distant gleam in the darkness, far too low to be a star.

I heard footsteps. Stopping beside me, Angus said, "Old Murdock must be wakeful tonight."

"Murdock?"

"He keeps the Macduveen falcons in the tower. A mute, Murdock is, although he hears well enough for a man of eighty."

"Does he live alone there?"

"Aye. Even though Murdock cannot abide women, they say that many years ago he had a wife and stepdaughter. But they are long since dead."

I thought of the old man alone in that ancient tower, hearing the falcons rustle on their perch, but no human voice, not even his own. "Does anyone fly the falcons?"

"Sir James used to. But the young laird seldom does, not even when he is here, and he is often away."

I said good night to Angus then, and went to the cobbler's hut. By the light of the candle Jenny had grudgingly allowed me, I put on my nightdress, a garment which it seemed to me I had stitched many years ago and in another world, instead of last winter in that snug little house on Job's Lane. I lay down on the straw pallet and blew out the candle. Gradually I was able to make out, by the starlight which fell through the hole in the roof, the room's one piece of furniture. It was my grandfather's cobbler's bench, over there beside the portmanteau and hand trunk. I had wanted to keep it here, even though one leg was broken. For a long while I lay awake, wondering what my grandfather had been like, and luxuriating in my solitude.

My solitary afternoon hours seemed equally blessed. In all sorts of weather—and it was a rare day that passed without periods of fog or rain—I roamed across the moors. Often I visited my father's grave, and then moved to the headland's edge to listen to the sea's thunder. Sometimes I wandered up narrow glens, where willows and scarlet-berried rowan trees bordered rushing streams, and the cool air had a ferny fragrance.

One lowering day I walked five miles to the village of Garlaig, a cluster of thatched stone huts around the stone kirk. In its churchyard I found the graves of my grandparents, Walter and Sara Logan. According to the dates on their gravestones, my grandfather had died when my father was twelve. My grandmother had lived until a year before my father had run away to fight in the Battle of Preston.

As I lingered there the sexton, a thin little man of sixty-odd, with bright inquisitive blue eyes under bushy brows, came out of the kirk and walked toward me. He said, looking at the gravestones, "Were they kin of yours?"

"My grandparents." I paused. "Do you know what they died of?"

"I do. I was not sexton here then, but it is in the parish record. It was lung fever that took them both, even though they died five years apart."

Lung fever. The scourge of the Gaels, my father had called it.

"Lung fever has taken many who served at Bowain Castle." With a kind of ghoulish melancholy, he showed me the graves of the wife and stepdaughter of Murdock, the falcon keeper. "First the mother went, and six months later the daughter." He pointed out the graves of Kenneth's parents. "Dead within a year of one another, and Kenneth still too young to be anything but stableboy." To my surprise, since she had not mentioned ever being married, he showed me the grave of Jenny's husband. "It was not lung fever that took this one. It was the drink. Died raving mad, they say." As I bade the sexton good-bye and turned away, I reflected that any man married to Jenny might have ended in a drunkard's grave.

It was on my way back from Garlaig that day that I had my first encounter with Murdock. I had gone perhaps a mile along the road, under rapidly thickening clouds, when the first isolated drops made small craters in the dust. With no more warning than that, the rain came in a wind-driven flood that soon had me soaked to the skin and gasping for breath. Even if I cut across the moors, I would not reach the kitchen in time to begin my late afternoon and evening tasks, not with the hem of my cloak heavy with mud and the wind blowing so hard that I had to force my way against it.

I was about to turn back to the kirk to wait out the storm when I looked to my left and saw, looming through the rain curtain, the ancient round tower on its low promontory. Turning off the road, I waded up the slope through sodden heather. As I climbed the promontory, I saw that a rough-coated Highland pony, head dropping under the downpour, stood in a wooden-railed pen beside the tower's rounded wall.

I pounded on the massive recessed door. After perhaps a minute I heard the scrape of wood on wood, and knew that he was sliding back the bar. I found myself looking into a wrinkled, white-bearded face on almost the same level as my own. Over his shoulder, by gray light that filtered through arrow slits, I could see the tethered birds moving restlessly on their long perch, some hooded, some with yellow eyes gleaming dully.

I smiled at the old man and said, "Could I wait here until the—"

Both his hands shot out and shoved my shoulders so violently that I almost fell. Stepping out into the rain, he seized my arm with one bony hand and shook it. He drew the forefinger of his other hand across his throat, and then pointed in the direction of the castle. His meaning was plain. If I, a loathed female, tried to invade his sanctuary again, he would kill me.

The threat was absurd. He was only a little taller than

I, perhaps only a few pounds heavier, and very old. But his eyes glared so wildly, and the soundless workings of his mouth were so grotesque, that I felt chilled by more than the rain.

I turned away and, head down, with the wind whipping my cloak, walked toward the castle. Even though the downpour dwindled and then ceased before I was halfway there, I arrived in the kitchen drenched and muddied. I stood before the hearth in my shift, hands extended to the warming blaze, while Jenny made a withering speech about addlepates who wander in the rain, leaving others to make supper and do the washing-up.

But seldom that summer had the weather been that harsh. Through mist and light rain and sunlight I had walked the moors and made my way up narrow glens. I had felt a growing love for this land I had never seen until a few weeks before. No, more than love; an eerie sense that I had always belonged here. Sometimes, in a shadowed glen, I had a sense that this same moss had been springy beneath my feet long ago, and the spray of that same waterfall cool against my face and arms.

And, as I have said, much of the time I was happy.

Today I had not finished my work before stealing a bit of sunlight and freedom. A number of house guests, including Clarence MacElvin and his handsome wife, had arrived that morning. Consequently I'd had to help Sally and Peg, the chambermaids, change bed linens. Arms full of sheets I intended to take down for Mag and me to launder, I moved along the hall toward the stairs spiraling down through the north tower. Once on the landing, I succumbed to temptation. It was such a lovely day, with fat little white clouds floating in a serene blue sky. Surely

I could spend a few minutes atop the north tower. And since these stairs were used only by servants, surely it would be all right to leave the linen here on the stone landing. I went up the stairs, paused for a moment at the next landing to look down a rush-strewn corridor stretching between two rows of long-unused rooms, and then continued up a shorter flight to a landing beneath the tower's roof. From there an iron ladder slanted upward to a trap door. When the castle was built, that door must have been some ponderous affair of stone or iron. But sometime during the centuries since, undoubtedly to admit light down the stairwell, it had been replaced by a hatch door of glass, its two halves secured by a hasp with an iron pin through it. I climbed the ladder, undid the hasp, and pushed the two halves of the door back until they rested on their hinges. Then I stepped out into sunlight and warm wind.

Now, as I stood at the parapet, my gaze strayed downward to that cowshed where my father had died. As always at the sight of it, I felt not only a stir of that old angry grief over the manner of his death, but a lingering, puzzled anxiety. *Had* someone fired at me that night?

Old Angus thought not. Less than forty-eight hours after my father's death, I returned to the castle from the first of my many late afternoon visits to my father's grave. The stable door had been open. At Angus's invitation I had gone inside and sat down on the three-legged stool he offered. It was there, with motes of dust and hay moving sluggishly in sunbeams slanting through cracks in the stable wall, that I told him of the pistol ball striking the cowshed, and of my failure to find it on the cobblestones either that night or when I returned to the castle late the next day after my exhausted sleep beside my father's grave.

"If the young laird fired that pistol," Angus said, "he meant not to hit you, but only to frighten, else you would be dead now, lass. Drink will ruin his hand and eye in time, but now he is still a marksman. I know, because I have set up targets for him on the moor."

Probably, he had gone on to say, the pistol had been fired at random by one of Sir Donald's drunken friends. It had happened before during such rowdy gatherings. "When the young scapegrace, whoever he was, saw that he had almost hit someone, he was afraid you would complain to her ladyship about it, and show her the pistol ball to give your story credit. And so he himself slipped down to the courtyard and took it. I'll warrant that was the way of it."

I had wanted to believe so. Since I had little choice but to stay in this place, or beg for my bread along the road, I wanted to believe that a drunken stranger had fired a pistol at random. Certainly I did not want to believe that it had been fired in deadly malice by Donald Macduveen, or by that saturnine-faced man who had dragged Donald away from me, or by Jenny, or Mag, or anyone else here.

Dismissing the thought of those first nightmarish hours at Bowain Castle, I lifted my gaze from the courtyard and looked across the strait. Over on Skye, a small cloud's shadow had touched a jagged peak, turning it from purple to deep blue. Had Charles Edward Stuart doubled back to hide somewhere over there among those crags? He had been on Skye, people said, in July. When the hunters drew close, a young woman named Flora MacDonald had helped him to escape back to the mainland by dressing him in woman's clothing and passing him off as her Irish maid, Betty Burke. (Flora MacDonald was said to be handsome. Had she appeared so, I wondered, in Charles Edward's eyes?)

Unless he had escaped to France within the last few days, or been taken prisoner, he was still somewhere here in the Highlands, a hunted quarry doubling and redoubling on his trail while all the hounds—English soldiers, local militiamen, English warships sailing up and down Loch Ness and among the Western Isles—bayed futilely after him.

That he was still at large had seemed to me inexplicable, until a conversation I had with Jenny one rainy and unseasonably chill August morning. While she and I knelt at the hearth baking bannocks and Mag swept the stone floor, Kenneth had come in to warm his hands at the hearth. English warships, he reported, had been on a wild-goose chase up to the outermost of the Western Isles, where it had been reported that Charles Edward was hiding. Instead of a prince, they had found a handful of bewildered men and women and children, subsisting miserably on the rocky isle with their goats and cattle, and so isolated from the rest of the world that they had never heard of King George, let alone Charles Edward Stuart.

I said, "But how is it they have not found him *someplace?*"

"Because everywhere he finds friends. They give him food and shelter, and warn him when it is best to move on," Jenny said, and then added, "Thank the merciful Lord."

I was so startled that I almost dropped the griddle. "But

he is a Catholic!"

"So he is, poor ignorant lad. And bad cess to those who follow him because he is a Papist. But he is a Scot, and the son of a rightful king, and the grandson of a crowned king. Besides, we Dissenters are strong enough to withstand any king, be he Catholic or Church of England."

Would I ever, I wondered, understand the Scottish and their contradictory loyalties? I said, "Charles Edward did not strike me as a man who would be intolerant in religious matters."

Jenny and Kenneth stared at me. Behind me, the sound of Mag's sweeping stopped. Jenny asked, "What would you know of such things?"

My chance meeting with Charles had been many weeks before. Surely it would do no harm to talk of it now. "Because I talked with him," I said, and described that daybreak encounter there by the river's bank.

Jenny said, "They say he is still of good heart. But surely he must grieve over the sorrows his enemies have brought to Scotland."

Now, standing in the sunlight atop the north tower, I thought of those sorrows. Here on Macduveen land, all was peaceful. But in Inverness, it was said, the jail was filled to suffocation with suspected Jacobite sympathizers and with defeated survivors of Culloden, many of them with untended wounds. So were the holds of prison ships anchored in Loch Ness and Moray Firth, awaiting orders to sail their wretched cargo to London for trial and for almost inevitable hanging, drawing, and quartering. And throughout the Highlands, except on lands owned by Scottish adherents of the London government, bands of soldiers roamed—hanging, shooting, raping. They went deep into the glens to burn huts, confiscate small stores of food, and drive off scrawny Highland cattle for sale to Lowland and English farmers, leaving the survivors of their raids to find what shelter they could in hillside caves.

A line of dark clouds had formed above Skye's mountains now. Soon they would sweep over the strait to blot out the afternoon sun. I turned, lowered myself to the iron ladder, and closed and secured the trap door. I descended the first spiral of stone steps, glanced briefly along the corridor between rooms used only for storage, and started down the second flight.

I was aware of sudden movement behind me. Before I could turn my head, something shoved me violently between the shoulder blades. I experienced that distorted time sense that comes with shock. It seemed to me that I hung in midair, body slanted forward, for at least two seconds before I toppled onto the stairs and began to slide. Time speeded up then. I clutched futilely at the smooth, curving walls, trying to stop my headfirst descent to that stone landing below.

With a suddenness that jarred every bone in my body, my fall was checked. I lay there with head and shoulders deep in a smothering softness.

Twelve

It took me several seconds to realize that I was still alive and could move. I got to hands and knees and then, shakily, to my feet, and stood staring down at the pile of bed linen which had saved my life.

Had the person who rushed at me from that dim corridor known that I had left a pile of sheets here? If so, his attack had been designed to shock and terrify, not to kill. And surely he must have been aware of the linen, if he had climbed up these stairs.

But what if he had not? What if someone in the courtyard, or in the row of outbuildings behind it, or on the moor sloping down from the castle's eastern wall, had seen me up there on the tower roof, and had slipped up the stairs through the other tower, the stairs reserved for gentry?

The gentry. I thought of Donald Macduveen, dragging me into his darkened bedchamber that first night. I thought of the pistol ball striking the wall of that shed where my father lay dying. Now I was sure that it had not been one of his drunken friends who had fired that pistol.

It had been Donald himself.

I began to tremble, not with fear, but rage. Did he, that fat wastrel, think he was some fourteenth-century baron, with the right to ravish any peasant girl who took his eye, and the right to terrorize her if she successfully resisted? If so, it was time someone told him of his error.

For a moment I was checked by the thought that if anyone was to give Sir Donald his comeuppance, it had best be someone in a less precarious situation than myself, a girl possessed of only two shillings, six pence. He was laird here. He had the legal right to drive me, not only from under his roof, but across the border of Macduveen lands, miles beyond the village of Garlaig. But I did not think that his mother, placid and self-centered as she was, would allow him to do that. And besides, I was too angry not to risk it.

I smoothed my hair and my dress, reflecting as I did so that there must be bruises on my body. Then, stepping around the pile of linen, I moved across the threshold into the carpeted corridor. Through the partially opened door at the end of the hall, the one that led to Lady Macduveen's sitting room and bedchamber, I could hear animated talk and laughter. I went to the door of Donald Macduveen's room and knocked.

For several seconds there was no answer. Had he joined his mother and her guests? Was he still in the corridor above? Or was he in his room, still breathless from his swift retreat down the other stairs and along this corridor? At last he called out, "Who is there?"

I said loudly, "Elizabeth Logan."

Several more seconds of silence. Then he opened the door, his round face expressionless above a dressing robe of silk tartan. "What do you want?"

To my annoyance, my voice shook. "I want to know why you pushed me down the staircase."

He said, with seeming astonishment, "Push you! Why, I could not bring myself to even touch you."

His retort was so unexpected that for a moment I was speechless. Then I said, with fury, "Not touch me! Why, my first night here—"

"That was then. Now is now." His scornful gaze dropped from my face to my hands. "If I had a taste for sun-browned wenches with lobster-red hands, I could find dozens."

I knew that it was his malice that spoke, and yet I felt a humiliated impulse to hide my hands behind my skirt. It was true that they were red and chapped. In the Job's Lane house I had kept a mixture of rosewater and glycerine in the kitchen. But here I had not the ingredients for such a lotion, nor would I have wanted to use it under Mag and Jenny's scornful gaze. And it was true that I had given little thought to my complexion as I washed clothes in the courtyard and, during my free afternoon hours, wandered through sun and rain over the moors. In my hand trunk there was a hat of leghorn straw, which my father had bought for me in Boston. But I would have looked absurd, a kitchenmaid wearing a hat. And besides, the man whom I had hoped would always find me pleasing to look at was an ocean away.

Nevertheless, I found that I still had vanity—vanity tender enough to be wounded by Donald Macduveen's sneer. I said thickly, "Never mind about my face and hands. I think you pushed me down those stairs."

"Probably no one pushed you. Probably you tripped.

Unless . . ." A slow smile spread over his face. "Unless it was Belzebub who pushed you. He likes to send people sprawling."

Belzebub, that giant deerhound of his. The beast seemed to roam wherever he chose. Often I had seen him padding along this corridor. Once in the courtyard he had come up behind me as I was carrying water from the well, and thrust his nose into one of the wooden buckets, startling me so that I dropped it onto the cobblestones.

I began to feel doubt. It was true that I had not heard footsteps before I hurtled down those stairs. Rather I had had just a sense of movement behind me. Had my assailant been a human moving on stocking feet, or Belzebub, the click of his claws inaudible over the rush-strewn stones of that upper corridor?

Smiling now, the laird of Bowain Castle stepped past me, faced the doorway to the southern tower, and gave a high-pitched whistle. Within seconds the huge, rough-coated animal emerged from the doorway and trotted toward us. He sniffed at my gown and then went into his master's room.

I said, in that shaking voice, "If it was the dog, then you must have been up there too. You signaled him to do it."

Donald seemed genuinely amused. "A prankster like Belzebub needs no signals. And do you think I would spend my time training him to push kitchen wenches down stairs?"

He went into his room and closed the door in my face. I stood there for a moment, my heart still pounding with anger, not just because of that plunge down through the north tower, but because of his sneer at my appearance. Had I become so unappealing? I did not know. My only mirror was a small one in my portmanteau, and I had not bothered to use it for weeks. True, when I helped Nan and Sally in the castle bedchambers, I sometimes caught a glimpse of myself in a mirror. But even if I had cared to risk their derision by pausing to inspect my image, I would not have done so. Always I was too resentful of those extra tasks, and too intent upon hurrying through them so that I could enjoy what was left of my afternoon freedom.

I moved away down the corridor and then, just before I reached the north tower entrance, halted at a closed door. That room, the elderly chambermaids had told me, was never used. Still, it might contain a mirror. I tried the iron doorknob. It resisted for a moment, and then turned with a grating sound. I slipped into the room and closed the door behind me.

Light that came through the tattered remains of yellow silk draperies showed me why this room was never used. It would have taken days to render it fit for a guest. Dust lay thick upon the torn and sagging yellow brocade canopy of the bed, and on its elaborately carved dark posts. On the carpet the dust was so thick that I could not discern its pattern. And a huge spiderweb, its dark weaver scuttling along one of its strands, hung between a bedpost and the tall back of an armchair, its upholstered seat so gray with dust that it might have been any color at all. A small hearth in the far wall still held the ashes of a long-dead fire.

As I stood there in the silence, I felt an odd stilling of all my senses. Then it came to me, just as it did at times in a glen murmurous with running water—that sense of familiarity, almost as if in some life lost to conscious memory I had known this room.

Arabella's room, I thought. Arabella, who had sinned the unpardonable sin of self-murder. Just as her drowned body had been deemed unfit to lie with those of shriven Christians, so the room where she had slept would be left to the dust and the spiders.

A gilt framed mirror hung on the wall above a narrow table, its legs hidden by a tattered, dusty skirt of some indiscernible pattern. Before the table stood a little chair of dark wood, graceful and feminine despite its coating of dust. Aware that I must be leaving footprints, I crossed the room.

The mirror's surface was dusty and flyspecked. With the lower edge of the tattered drapery, I cleaned the glass's surface and then, bending slightly, looked at my reflection.

It was true that my hair, often unprotected even by a shawl when I roamed the countryside, now had streaks bleached to a lighter yellow. It was true that my complexion was no longer pink and white, and that there was a sprinkling of freckles across the bridge of my nose. But my skin could not be called "sun-browned." Rather the sun had altered it to a shade resembling that of pale gold. My eyes under my sun-bleached brows were as blue as ever, and my mouth if anything was pinker than in the days when I used to go about the streets of Southampton, shawled or bonneted, and wearing a dress that bore no stain of kitchen grease. I no longer looked like the daughter of a man who knew Latin and Greek. But neither had I turned into the leathery hag that Donald Macduveen's words had conjured up. I lingered for another moment, inspecting a red streak along my jaw that no doubt soon would be a bruise, and then moved to the door.

Hand on the iron knob, I took a last look around the room, trying to picture Arabella asleep beneath that now tattered canopy, or standing by the window with its view of the moor falling away to the road. I could not, since I had no idea whether she had been dark or fair, tall or short. Lady Macduveen had come to Bowain Castle several years after Arabella's death. Of all the servants in the castle only Jenny and Kenneth had been here when Arabella was alive, and Kenneth had been only a child. When I once questioned him about her, all he could recall was that he had considered her "bonnie," and that when his father was dying and his mother already ill, she had brought food and extra blankets to their croft. As for Jenny, she had flatly refused to discuss the young woman who, thirty-one years before, had doomed herself "to eternal hellfire."

I left the room, crossed the corridor, and stood looking at two portraits which hung there on the wall. The artist had depicted Sir James Macduveen as a grave-looking young man of about twenty-five, brown-haired, and with a firm, unsmiling mouth. His brother Malcolm's portrait must have been painted shortly before his mount had thrown him to his death, because in it he appeared to be a youth of about twenty, also brown-haired, but with a smile that held a hint of lighthearted recklessness. Surely Arabella's portrait must have hung beside those of her brothers at one time. Probably it had been destroyed after her suicide, or hidden away up there in one of those rooms used for storage. I went to the north tower, gathered up the pile of linen, and descended to the kitchen.

Mag, seated on a stool with a knife in one hand and a

turnip in the other, raised her head to look at me. Jenny turned away from the hearth and put her hands on her hips. "So it is her ladyship, is it? And what has her ladyship been doing above all this time?" Then, in a different tone: "What happened to your face?"

I dropped the linen into the deep wooden handcart which stood beside the hearth. "Someone—something—pushed me down the steps. I think it was that horrible great dog of Sir Donald's."

Mag gave a snort of laughter. Jenny looked at me with that strange, closed expression I had often seen on her broad face. "This seems an unlucky place for you. First a pistol ball almost strikes you. And now you come near to breaking your neck on the stairs."

Angus, not I, had told her about the pistol ball. Twice before now she had referred to it. "Perhaps it would be best," she said, "that you find work elsewhere."

That might have been advice. It might have been a taunt or a veiled threat. Her flat tone made it impossible to be sure. I looked at her, wondering not for the first time how she really regarded me. Sometimes, as now, I felt that in spite of her grudging appreciation of my work, her hostility toward me, the granddaughter of that secret Papist, Sara Logan, had modified itself not one whit. As I drew the handcart toward the kitchen doorway, I said, in what I am sure Jenny considered a saucy tone, "I will go somewhere else if I choose to."

It was an idle boast, of course. Where could I go? No one in Garlaig was rich enough to hire a servant. Two shillings, six pence would not buy my way to Inverness, where I might find work. And I would have to be desperate indeed before I set out to make my way on foot through a Scotland filled with roving bands of soldiers, many of whom seemed to feel that they could do as they liked with any defenseless man or woman they found.

Out in the courtyard I drew the cart to the big wooden washtub sitting beside the well, and then seized the windlass to lower the bucket.

I had a distinct sense of someone's eyes upon me. Hand dropping away from the windlass, I turned and looked up at the castle's rear wall. A dark-haired man stood at one of the long windows looking down at me. His immobility gave me an impression of concentrated intentness. At first I thought he was Clarence MacElvin. But no. He appeared shorter, and somewhat younger than the man who had grasped Donald Macduveen's coat collar and hauled him out into the corridor. Probably he was Clarence Mac-Elvin's younger brother, the one whom, it was said, Arabella Macduveen would have preferred to marry.

The man turned away and disappeared. Grasping the windlass, I lowered the bucket into the well.

Thirteen

The Macduveens' guests left late the next afternoon. I saw them leave. Returning from a solitary two hours on the moor, I paused just outside the courtyard's rear archway. A coach was drawn up in the entrance tunnel. As I watched, the aged footman handed Clarence MacElvin's handsome brunette wife into the coach, then a plump lady of fifty-odd with graying red hair, then Clarence MacElvin, and then the man who had looked down at me from the window above the courtyard. Jenny had confirmed my guess that he was Clarence's younger brother Ian. The red-haired lady was his wife. Mag, with that snorting laugh of hers, had added a bit of information about the younger MacElvin's wife. She was "daft" about her husband, even though they had been married for almost thirty years, and "jealous as a witch."

The balmy weather broke that night. I awoke at first light, feeling chilled, and saw a mixture of rain and sleet pelting through the broken roof. For three days the weather was so bad that each afternoon, after a too-brief outing on the moor, I returned reluctantly to sit by the kitchen hearth until it was time for my evening tasks. I still slept in the hut, under my cloak as well as an additional blanket, smelling of horse, which Angus had supplied. (Jenny, affronted by my stubborn desire for privacy, had refused to ask the upstairs servants to give me a blanket from the store of household bedding.) But soon, I knew, the cold would drive me out of the hut. Yes, even if Kenneth carried out his oft-postponed intention of mending the roof. Through the long winter I would not only spend my working hours with the often-censorious Jenny and the always-hostile Mag. At night I would lie in the kitchen corner aware of Mag only a few feet away, perhaps awake and entertaining God only knew what thoughts in that brain behind the too-low forehead. On her privileged spot before the hearth, Jenny would make the cavernous kitchen resound with her snores.

One morning I awoke to see that the patch of sunrise sky revealed by the broken roof was clear. What was more, the air seemed a little warmer than it had for several days. I had begun to dress when I saw that someone had slipped a folded sheet of paper under the door. Incredulously—for who in this place could have written to me?—I picked it up and unfolded it. The note, written in a strong masculine hand, set my pulses to racing. It read:

Elisabeth,
   If you recal meating a new friend one daybrake last June beside a river, will you help that friend now? We nede bred, chees, meat. Brandey if possible. We are in Bowain Wood. Enter wood at stone cross. Whair path branches go to *left*. One of us will meat you. If you can not bring brandey, wine will do. Come at dusk.
                                        Your svt.,
                                        E. C.

So after all these months, and all the perils and hardships he must have endured, he had remembered my name, and that my father and I were bound for Bowain Castle. But it was the bad spelling, more than the use of my name, which convinced me of the note's genuineness. Angus had told me that the Prince was said to speak three languages—Italian, French, and English—and to be unable to spell in any of them.

As to why he was now hiding on Macduveen lands, I had no idea. When I saw him, I would ask him. Because of a certainty I intended to go to him, bringing the provisions his note requested. Swiftly I finished dressing, thrust the note down the bodice of my dress, and went to the kitchen.

By midmorning, I saw that I would not have to wait until dusk to go to Bowain Wood. Undoubtedly Charles Edward had wanted me to come there at an hour when there was less chance of my being observed. But now heavy fog had rolled across the strait to the mainland, and settled down in the almost windless air. For once I was glad that the morning had not kept its bright promises. Far better that I leave at my usual midafternoon hour, rather than absent myself from my evening tasks, and thus have to make up some explanation for an irate Jenny upon my return.

A little past three that afternoon I moved through the dense fog blanketing the moorland which sloped down from the castle's front wall. To anyone watching from a window, I must long since have been swallowed up by the gray smother. No one would know which direction I took. The shawl-wrapped bundle of provisions, which I had smuggled out of the courtyard under my cloak, I now carried in my hand.

It had been easy to assemble those provisions. When Gerald appeared in the kitchen to take up the wine for Lady Macduveen and Sir Donald's dinner, I had volunteered to fetch it from the cellar. Along with the wine, I had brought up a bottle of brandy, and hidden it behind the churn in the larder. During the next hour, taking advantage of moments when I was observed by neither Jenny nor Mag, I added a round loaf of bread, cheese, and a joint of mutton to my hidden hoard. Jenny would miss the mutton, if not the bread and cheese, but that did not matter. She would blame it on Belzebub, who more than once had invaded the kitchen to make off with a joint or a fowl. Shortly before three, when the washing-up had been done and Jenny and Mag stood gossiping with Kenneth at the courtyard well, I hastily wrapped the provisions in one of the muslin cloths used to cover rising bread. The bundle hidden under my cloak, I had sauntered back to my stone hut. There, before leaving the castle by the courtyard's rear archway, I had made the bundle stouter by wrapping it in a red woolen shawl from the hand trunk.

I had reached the road now. I turned left. With a sense that I walked inside a little hollow scooped out of the fog, which moved along with me, I walked two miles. Then I saw, at the right-hand side of the road, the ancient stone cross which, some people said, had been placed there nearly a thousand years ago by Irish missionaries from the island of Iona. A few yards beyond it lay the entrance to the path into Bowain Wood.

Momentarily I hesitated. None of my wanderings had taken me into that wood. It was not that I had believed that rascally carter's story about the wolves. The very slyness in his voice told me that he had hoped to impose upon my gullibility as a newcomer. Beside, Angus had told me that the last wolf in this part of the Highlands had been seen—and shot by a sheepherder—more than twenty years before. Rather it was that, when out of doors, I like to be able to look up and see clouds or sunlight. Even in the narrowest of glens there was always a ribbon of sky overhead. But in that dense wood I would be moving beneath a many-layered canopy of leaves and branches.

I did find the grayness much darker there among the interlaced trees. All around me moisture dripped from branches onto dead leaves, with a pattering sound which resembled that of light rain. Now and then I caught a whiff of acrid peat smoke. Was the fire in some crofter's hut beyond the woods? Or had the fugitive and his friends risked kindling a fire against the gray chill?

Here was the branching path. I set down my bundle, took the note from the bosom of my dress, and made sure that I was to take the path bearing to the left. I picked up the bundle and went on. The smell of peat smoke was stronger now. Yes, surely the fire was somewhere here in the woods.

Through the drip of moisture I could hear something else—a faint trickling sound, as of sluggishly moving water. Probably, just beyond that bend in the path, I would find a bridge spanning a shallow stream, its course half choked by dead leaves and fallen branches.

I turned the bend. As yet I could see no bridge, although the trickling sound, oddly diffused now, seemed louder. But then, dense fog plays strange tricks with sound. I went on for a yard or so, over ground that sloped gently downward.

And then my right foot, stepping forward, plunged halfway to the knee into a viscous coldness. Thrown off balance, I fell forward. My arms, which I instinctively thrust out in front of me to break the force of my fall, went elbow-deep into that black, ill-smelling substance. Somehow I pulled my arms free and stood erect, aware of trickling sounds all around me in the gray smother. I had blundered into a bog, I realized now, and that trickling sound was made by sluggish streamlets cutting channels into the mire. I turned and, with the mire sucking at my feet, tried to get back onto solid ground. But apparently, confused by the fog and my own panic, I had moved in the wrong direction, because after four laborious steps I was still in that fetid softness, and at each step I had sunk deeper.

I forced myself to stand still. Sunk in that black muck to well over the knees now, I threw back my head and screamed again and again.

Fourteen

There was no sound except my own screams and, when I paused for breath, the slow trickle of the streamlets. Charles Edward was not in these woods. No one was. The note luring me into this bog had been a murderous hoax. And I was going to die, sinking deeper and deeper into this filthy stuff until it choked my mouth and nostrils and closed over my head. Again I began to struggle, trying to free my legs, groping wildly about me with my hands in hope of touching firm earth or some such solid object as a fallen tree trunk.

I heard the muffled pound of running feet. A man's shape loomed dimly through the mist, and a voice with a rich Scottish burr called, "You, there! Stop thrashing about. You will only sink deeper."

I heard the crack of a branch parting from a tree. The branch's leafy end struck the surface of the bog so close to me that leaves brushed my face. My hands, groping through twigs, found the branch's central stem, rough-barked and perhaps three inches in circumference, and fastened around it. I felt my rescuer begin to pull. My legs came free with a sucking sound. On my stomach, and holding my head above the soft, ill-smelling earth, I was drawn to solid ground.

Hands lifted me to my feet. As I stood there, heart still pounding, I heard him say, "Why, it is a lass!"

I looked into a sandy-bearded, vaguely familiar face. After a second or two I recognized him. His had been one of the faces looking down at me when I awoke beside the riverbank that morning last June. He must have recognized me at almost the same moment, because he asked, in a voice rough with suspicion, "What are you doing here?"

My screams had left my throat feeling raw. "I received a note. It was signed with Charles Edward's initials, and—"

"That is a lie! The Prince has sent no note." From the dismay that immediately crossed his face, I knew that he wished he had made some less revealing reply.

"I know," I said. "But I thought it was from him." I reached inside the bosom of my dress. Yes, the folded paper was still there. With muddy fingers I extended the note to him.

"I do not know my letters. What does it say?"

I replaced the note inside my dress. "It told me to bring food and drink to Bowain Wood. It said to go to the left where the path branched."

"He sent you no note. But now that you are here, what the de'il am I to do with you?" I had the feeling that his sense of dilemma was so strong that he wished he had left me in the bog.

"Come on," he said finally. "Walk ahead of me. And don't try to run for it."

I felt an impulse toward hysterical laughter. Even if I had wanted to, how could I, my clothing weighted with muck, hope to outdistance him?

We moved back to where the path branched, and took the right-hand turning. Still walking ahead of my rescuer, I turned one bend in the path, then another. Up ahead a tall, striding figure took shape in the mist. He halted in front of me. "Why, it is the American lady!"

There he stood, the great-great-great-grandson of Mary Queen of Scots, still with red-gold hair untrimmed, still in the old black coat and kilt, still bare of foot and leg. In his brown eyes sympathy struggled with mirth. He added, "And it is a sorry state you are in, too. It seems you have brought half the bog with you."

"Yes, it is the American lass," my rescuer said. "And why has she been snooping in these woods, eh?"

I said swiftly to Charles, "Someone sent me a note." I held the paper out to him. "I thought it was from you."

He took it. "We will talk about that later. Right now we will go back to the fire."

We went around another bend in the path and emerged into a small grassy clearing. Beside a rude wooden hut, its roof thatched with heather, a small fire burned. An old man and a boy of about fourteen, neither of whom I had ever seen before, stood warming themselves at the pale yellow flames.

Charles said, "See what Sandy fished out of the bog!" Then, to me: "Best go into the hut and rid yourself of those clothes. There is a clean shirt of mine hanging on the peg. Put that on, wrap a blanket around you, and come back to the fire."

As I hesitated, shivering with cold, he added, "All right. Keep your shift if you must. But throw that muddy cloak and your dress out onto the grass. Johnny here"—he nodded toward the boy—"will wash them in the pool." He gave my shoulder a gentle shove. "Go, Elizabeth. Do you want to catch a chill?" So, just as I had believed when I read that spurious note, Charles had remembered my name.

I stepped into the hut and closed the door. Gray light filtering between the rough boards which formed its walls showed a straw pallet, with two brown blankets folded neatly at one end. Otherwise the room was empty except for the Prince's clean but worn-looking white woolen shirt, swaying from the peg on the door, and a stone jug, of the sort that usually holds brandy, in one corner. Evidently only the Prince slept here. His even hardier guardians, apparently, bedded down under the sky.

I took off my mire-weighted cloak and dress. My shift, although wet, was comparatively clean. Opening the door narrowly, I tossed my cloak and dress onto the grass. Then I wrapped myself in one of the blankets and moved toward the fire.

My rescuer and the old man had disappeared. The boy, with my cloak and dress over his arm, was moving away through the trees. On the opposite side of the fire, I noticed, the men had already set up a drying rack, a stout pole stretching several feet above the ground and supported at each end by a notched tree branch. Charles sat on a log beside the fire. He stood up as I approached. "Sit as close to the fire as you can."

When I had settled myself on the log, he reached behind it and brought up a stone jug and a pewter cup. "Brandy," he said, spilling amber liquid into the cup. "It is a sovereign remedy for ladies who have been floundering in bogs, and for much else, too."

He was right. After the first sip of the fiery liquid, I felt warmth begin to spread through me. Reaching again behind the log, he brought up a bottle. "Highland whiskey," he explained. "I have developed a taste for it. He drank directly from the bottle, recorked it, and placed the bottle behind the log.

"Now," he said, as he sat down beside me, "who brought you that—"

He broke off. The boy Johnny was coming toward us, my wet garments over his arm. He twisted my cloak and dress until all possible moisture was wrung from them, and then spread them on the pole. "Thank you," I said. The boy grinned at me and walked away through the trees.

Charles said, "Who brought you that note?"

"I don't know. When I woke up in my hut this morning, I saw it had been pushed under the door."

I saw puzzlement come into his eyes at the word "hut." But all he said was, "Who wrote it, do you suppose?"

"I don't know that, either."

I had been asking myself that question, of course. Who could have known that such a note would send me into these woods? Obviously it had to be someone who knew of my previous meeting with Charles Edward. Only Jenny and Kenneth and Mag had been in the kitchen when I told of that episode. But undoubtedly they had repeated it to the old footman and the two chambermaids, and they in turn might have told Lady Macduveen and Sir Donald. For that matter, I could imagine Sir Donald and Lady Macduveen regaling any or all of their guests with the story of their kitchenmaid's encounter with Charles Edward Stuart.

Perhaps Donald Macduveen was vicious enough to try to send me to my death in that bog. But there might be others in whom, for some reason unknown to me, I had aroused such enmity or fear that they wished me dead. Clarence MacElvin, my first night at Bowain Castle, had evinced a puzzling amount of curiosity about a mere serving wench. So had his brother Ian, that day he stared down at me from a rear window.

Could any of my fellow servants have written that note? I did not know which, if any, of them was literate. But Kenneth and Angus and Mag and Jenny, I had learned, had each had Dissenting parents and grandparents. My father had told me that such families, with their fierce determination to allow no priestly intercession between themselves and the word of God, usually insisted that every family member be able to read Holy Writ.

Charles Edward's laugh broke in on my thoughts. "One thing is certain. My reputation as a poor scholar must have traveled far and wide. But the fellow who wrote that note pulled too long a bow. Even I know how to spell brandy. Did you, by the way, start out with brandy?"

"Yes. And cheese and meat and bread."

"All lost in the bog, I suppose."

"Yes." Along with my good red shawl.

He sighed. "We have no great need for the food. But I mourn that brandy."

For a while there was no sound except the faint crackle of the fire. Then I said, "I have been thinking about all this. Whoever wrote that note must have known that one of you might hear my screams and come to help me."

His brown eyes were suddenly grave. "I think he did not know. I was supposed to move on from these woods two nights ago, with some people named MacDonald. Sandy, though, was stricken with some sort of fever. He did not want to be left behind, and since he has been a good friend to me—no friend could be better—I sent the MacDonalds on ahead. Sandy and I and the boy and old Ferguson will leave tonight."

He paused and then said, "Probably the story went around that the MacDonalds had been seen leaving Bo-wain Wood, and that I must be with them. Whoever sent that note expected that you would be entirely alone in here."

And if I had come "at dusk," as the note instructed, it would have been completely dark under those interlaced trees. Once I had blundered into the bog, I would have had almost no chance of saving myself.

I wrenched my mind away from the thought of that black muck smothering my mouth and nose and then clos-ing over my head. I said, "How is it that you are here? I would have thought that Macduveen lands were the last place you would come."

"Because the Macduveens support the present English government? But that is why this is a good place to hide. There are no bands of soldiers roaming Macduveen and MacElvin lands."

"But on Macduveen lands someone besides a soldier may try to collect that thirty thousand pounds." That chronic wastrel, Sir Donald Macduveen, for instance.

"And risk a knife between his shoulder blades some dark night?"

After a moment I said, "I see." If even such a fanatical anti-Papist as Jenny could feel sympathy for the fugitive, it was easy to imagine how determined his followers would be to avenge his capture. "Still," I said, "I cannot understand why you have not been caught. For months now, your movements must have been common talk throughout the Highlands. I know they are up at the castle. And yet you are still free."

He smiled. "Knowing where I am rumored to be is one thing. Finding me still there is another. Always there are those to warn me when Redcoats or militiamen come into view. Right now watchers are stationed near the edges of the wood. It was only because of the fog that you were able to slip past without being seen."

Yes, helpers everywhere, including a young woman named Flora MacDonald. I said, "You mentioned some people named MacDonald. Are they kin to Miss Flora MacDonald?"

He laughed. "So you have heard of her and her Irish maid, have you? Lord, I will never understand how you women get about in skirts. More than once I tripped and nearly fell flat. But as for her being kin to these Mac-Donalds, or they kin to each other, who can say? You know how it is with a Highland clan. The members call themselves by the same name and claim common ancestors centuries back. But whether two MacDonalds or two Mac-Intyres are fifth cousins, or five hundredth cousins, or no cousin at all, they cannot tell, nor does it seem to matter."

I nodded. To my surprise, I had learned that Kenneth and Jenny and Mag had all been born with the surname Macduveen, although any blood kinship that they might have with each other, let alone with the lairds of Bowain Castle, had been lost in the mists of time.

"What is Miss Flora MacDonald like?"

He said soberly, "She is a very fine, brave lady."

From his tone I knew that no matter what romantic ballads might be written for this or future generations to sigh over, Flora MacDonald had been just that to Charles Stuart—a fine lady, who had won his gratitude and respect, but had brought no amorous sparkle to his eye. It was small of me, I know, but I found my discovery pleasant.

He said, "Do you feel calm enough to talk about it now?" When I looked at him questioningly, he went on, "Who could possibly have wanted to send you to your death, Elizabeth?"

"There's—there's the laird, Sir Donald."

"Sir Donald Macduveen? But he is your kinsman!" As he spoke, I saw his eyes go to my hands, coarsened and reddened by the roughest sort of indoor and outdoor work in all sorts of weather.

I shook my head. "What my father had always told me was not true." I drew a deep breath and then, my words tumbling over one another, described the night of my father's death, and my life at Bowain Castle since then.

When I stopped speaking, he said something in a foreign tongue and then smiled at me. "In Italian that means poor little fledgling." His smile vanished. "The world has not been too kind to either of us these past months, has it?"

"I have not found them as bad as one might think, at least much of the time. I am young and strong, and I have enough to eat, and I have shelter. And I can always hope that my life will change for the better."

"True. And that is more than many in Scotland can say tonight." He looked suddenly tired, and much older. I knew he was thinking, not of himself, but of those who wandered aimlessly, their poor houses burned, their cattle and small stores of food gone. I knew that he must be thinking of the men in prison hulks and in Inverness jails, and of the wretched hundreds—once fiercely proud Highlanders, however poor—who had been shipped to the British Colonies in North America and the West Indies to be sold as bond servants.

Looking at his face, I wondered if he felt that nothing had been worth all that suffering. Not the gallant landing in the Highlands, nor the rallying of the Jacobites around his red and gold standard, nor that first triumphal march south.

He straightened his shoulders and then, with a forced-looking smile, turned to me. "And is returning to your American village one of your hopes, Elizabeth?"

"To America, perhaps." But not to my village. Never would I want to walk among those who had driven my father, almost penniless, from their midst.

"I wish I could help you. But as you see, it is all I can do to help myself." Again he smiled. "But I think we will meet at some future time, when we are both in better fortune."

His smile turned wry. "Not at the Court of St. James, I fear, at least not for some time. But perhaps at my father's court in Rome, although even as brightly plumaged a fledgling as you would begin to droop in such a gloomy place as that."

"You did not like growing up there?"

"In that dreary old palace the Pope bestowed upon us, with all those aging exiles talking and talking about the Stuart restoration, and concocting plots that came to nothing? I think it was because of that endless, empty talk that

I finally became rash enough to . . ."

He broke off and then said, "But we have more pressing matters to discuss. You must leave Bowain Castle, Elizabeth, as soon as you can."

"I know." I had been thinking about that even as I walked ahead of my suspicious rescuer, Sandy. Those first two episodes which had endangered my life might have been accidents. But that note had been no accident. Exactly where I would go I did not know, but surely Angus knew of some family in Garlaig who would be willing to shelter me, at least temporarily. I would return to the castle to get the portmanteau and hand trunk and the few coins in my purse. But sometime after dark, when I was sure no one would be observing me, I would leave.

In the next moment I learned I would not have to consult Angus, after all. Charles Edward tugged a tarnished metal button loose from his coat. "There is a couple in Garlaig named Lewis. Mrs. Lewis will recognize this button. She sewed it on for me. Her husband is a carter. Tell them that I wish him to take you to Inverness." Bitterness came into his voice. "Business is brisk there, what with all the English soldiers and the sailors from the warships. You should have no trouble finding work in someone's shop or household."

I let go of the blanket long enough to take the button. "And now you had best go," he said. "It will be dark soon."

He gathered my cloak and dress from the pole and, carrying them, walked with me to the hut. I went inside, and he handed my garments in to me. They were still damp, but my shift, warmed by my body and by the fire's heat, was now dry, and so I would not be too uncomfortable. I dressed swiftly, and thrust the precious button deep into the pocket of my cloak.

When I emerged from the hut, he stood beside the fire in the fading light, gaze fixed on the flames that now showed a deeper color. At my appoach he turned, smiled, and then, taking my right hand, raised it to his lips. When he released it, he said, "I saw you trying to fold the blanket over your hands, Elizabeth. Do you fear you now look like a kitchen drudge? You do not. In fact, yours is still the most pleasant face to look upon that I have seen."

I smiled. "In all your travels?"

"In all my travels."

He took my face between his hands and kissed me on the lips. Perhaps it was just the loneliness of those past months, but at the touch of his warm lips I felt a response that left me shaken. Evidently he experienced something of the same sort, because when he released me, I saw that his eyes had darkened.

He said abruptly, "You had best go." Turning, he gave a soft whistle. After a moment the old man and the boy and Sandy emerged from the wood. Turning back to me, Charles said, "Johnny will see you to the road. Good-bye, Elizabeth, until we next meet."

I did not believe we would, but I smiled and said, "Until then." I turned and followed the boy across the clearing and into the wood. He left me where the path joined the road near the ancient stone cross.

It was fully dark by the time I entered the castle courtyard through the rear archway. The torches had been lit above both archways, showing me that a coach, the same

129

one in which the MacElvin brothers and their wives had departed several days before, again stood in the entrance tunnel.

I had intended, before going to the kitchen, to change my still-damp dress for my green muslin, even though I knew that the sight of me in anything but Mag's too-large blue homespun would annoy Jenny. What matter that I annoyed her, either with my dress or my belated return to the kitchen, when I intended to leave this place within a few hours? But as I turned to my hut, I saw Jenny hurrying toward me.

"You are wanted in Lady Macduveen's sitting room at once."

I said, astonished, "Why?" Except for my first night here, I had never been in Lady Macduveen's rooms.

"I do not know."

Perhaps she did not, with certainty. But I am sure that she had guessed. As she stood there, her manner was no longer harsh, but strangely unsure.

I said, "I had intended to change my dress."

To my amazement she said, "That would be best. But hurry. Clarence and Ian MacElvin and their wives are there, and they are all waiting."

Fifteen

The door to Lady Macduveen's rooms stood partly open. As soon as I knocked, I heard quick footsteps. Ian MacElvin opened the door wide. His face, younger and fuller than that of his brother Clarence, held an expression that stunned me. His dark eyes beamed, and his smile had a warm, almost tremulous quality.

He said, "Come in, Elizabeth." As I stepped past him into the mingled light of the fire and of wax tapers in wall sconces, I threw a sweeping look around me. Lady Macduveen, flanked by the two Mrs. MacElvins, sat on a sofa which stood at right angles to the fire. Sir Donald lounged beside the fireplace, one elbow propped on the black marble mantel. Clarence MacElvin sat beside a small table against one wall, his fingers drumming on its dark polished surface.

In the far corner, in Highland dress, stood an old man I had never seen before, nervously turning his bonnet in his hands.

Lady Macduveen said, "We have something to tell you, Elizabeth."

Elizabeth, not Betty. I looked at her more closely. Even though her lips smiled, her prominent brown eyes revealed an unwonted agitation.

Ian MacElvin crossed to the table where his brother sat. On the table close to Clarence MacElvin's drumming fingers stood a gilt-framed canvas, its face to the wall. Ian turned it around.

I stood motionless.

As a child I had heard some adult say that everyone has, or has had, a duplicate somewhere among the earth's millions, and that to come face to face with one's duplicate presaged death. Perhaps that childhood memory was the reason why I felt a chill ripple down my body.

Not that the young woman in the portrait was my mirror image. For one thing her costume—a blue silk gown, with a bodice insert of lighter blue, and lace sleeve ruffles falling from just above the elbows halfway to the wrist— belonged to a fashion I could not remember from even my earliest years. For another, her hair was a shade darker than mine. Her rounded chin had a dimple, and at one corner of her smiling mouth there was a tiny mole, or perhaps a beauty spot. I have no mole, and no dimple. But otherwise, feature for feature, the face looking out at me from the canvas was my own.

Before anyone spoke, I knew who she had been. The girl who had slept in that bed beneath the tattered yellow canopy, and whose body, long since turned to dust, occupied that other lonely grave up there in the grassy clearing. Even now, in the first dazed moment after I had looked into her pictured face, I had room to wonder how it was that she, in the bloom of her youth, and surrounded by so much magical loveliness, could have walked into that loch.

Ian MacElvin, too, was looking at the pictured face. "At my request, Lady Macduveen had the storerooms searched until that portrait was found." There was tenderness in his voice and in his dark eyes that looked close to tears. "The girl in it was seventeen, and still unmarried when she sat for it. Elizabeth do you know who she was?"

Even to my own ears my voice had an odd, hushed quality. "I think she was Arabella Macduveen." I paused. "And I think I look so much like her because she was my great-aunt. My father was her brother Malcolm's son, his—his illegitimate son." I turned to face him. "Is that not the truth?"

He looked startled. "It is. But how did you know it?"

"Because until I came here I always believed that my father's father was Malcolm Macduveen. My father had told not only me that, but my mother, and everyone else in our village in America." I paused, and then added painfully, "What he did not tell me was that he was illegitimate. He could not bring himself to tell me that even on the night he died."

But he almost had. "Part of what I have always told you was true," he had said. "I am sure of it. You are my surety."

How old was I when my father first noticed the startling resemblance which confirmed his belief that we both possessed Macduveen blood? Had I been twelve? Thirteen? However old I was, I felt sure that even before that his claim to Macduveen ancestry had not been a mere fantasy, made up out of the whole cloth. Perhaps when he was so small that the incident had been lost to his conscious memory, he had heard some revealing conversation between his sempstress mother and the shoemaker who had married her. Perhaps he had heard his mother praying to the saints for forgiveness for her sin. Whatever the reason, long before I was born he must have been at least halfway convinced that his bloodline gave him a rightful claim to his elegant manners and his taste for fine clothes.

Ian was looking at me, still with that moist-eyed tenderness. I knew that it was not for me. It was for a girl long dead, a girl who had married, not him, but that silent brother of his who sat staring expressionlessly at the wall. "But, child, why did you not tell someone here that you believed yourself to be of Macduveen blood?"

"Because I no longer believed it. On—on the road up to the castle the night we came here, my father confessed that he had lied to me all my life. He had not grown up here as Sir James Macduveen's nephew. Instead he had been a potboy, and his mother the castle sempstress. I do not know for certain why he did not tell me that he nevertheless believed the shoemaker his mother married had not been his real father. But I think he did it for the sake of his mother's memory, and for my sake too. He'd had to tell me that—that I was the daughter of a fraud. He did not want to risk leaving me burdened also with the belief that my grandmother had been a wanton."

Ian said gently, "She was not that."

"I am sure she was not. But my father was dying. Perhaps he found he had not the strength to give me a true picture of his mother. And so he chose to have me believe that he himself had been the son of the man who married her." I hesitated. "Aside from my—my appearance, do you have any proof that—"

"Yes. After I saw you in the courtyard that day last week, I made it my business to find proof." He paused. "Do you know what your grandmother's maiden name was?"

I frowned, trying to remember. "It is on her tombstone in the graveyard beside the kirk. I think the name on the stone is Sara Fraser Logan."

He nodded. "I too went to the graveyard in Garlaig. The kirk's sexton told me that according to the parish records she had come from a family of crofters near Mallaig. I went there, and found that one of her younger brothers was still alive."

At his nod, the old man with the worn Highland plaid draped over his shoulder came hesitantly forward. "Elizabeth, this is Alex Fraser. Now, Alex, tell her what you told me."

The gnarled fingers clutched the bonnet tightly now. His face was flushed above his grizzled beard, and his eyes, faded blue ones, held the shame of a memory he must have thought long buried in the past. "My sister Sara came here to be sempstress many years ago. Before the turn of the century, it was. That one"—he nodded toward the portrait—"was a wee lass only a few years out of the cradle then, but her brother Sir James was twenty-two and already the laird, and her brother Malcolm was almost twenty." He stopped, his Adam's apple working.

I averted my gaze for a moment from his embarrassed face. "My grandmother's brother," I thought. What a divided heritage I had. On one side, dwellers in crofts. On the other, the lairds of Bowain Castle. I wanted to say, "I am glad and proud you are my great-uncle." Without crofter blood, I might not have survived these past few months. But of course I could not tell him that, not with those others listening, and not when he already found it hard enough to tell his story.

"My sister came home to the croft one day," he said. "She had caught young Malcolm's eye, and she had found him too pleasing to rebuff, and anyway, she was with child."

Again turning the bonnet between his hands, he went on to say that the Frasers had loaned money to some hard-pressed crofters named Logan. Their eldest son, Walter, a shoemaker by trade, was still unmarried. "We struck a bargain. If Walter Logan would marry my sister, we would cancel the Logans' debt to us. He did marry her, and came to Bowain Castle as shoemaker."

He looked at me earnestly. "Your grandmother was no wanton. She spent the rest of her life repenting her sin."

I nodded, remembering Jenny's scornful account of the hidden crucifix, the prayers to the saints. Apparently the fact that my grandmother had escaped the world's censure had only intensified her need to atone in the sight of God.

Jenny. Of all the people now at Bowain Castle, both gentry and servants, she and Kenneth alone had been here thirty-odd years ago, when Arabella was still alive. Kenneth had been only a child then, too young to retain any memory of my great-aunt except that she had been "bonnie," and kind to his parents. True, perhaps the faint puzzlement in his eyes that first day he saw me had sprung from some confused recollection of Arabella's face. But if so, apparently it had not been strong enough to emerge into his full consciousness.

Jenny, though, had been a mature woman at the time of

Arabella's suicide. Surely she had realized at first sight of me that I was of Macduveen blood. Why, then, had she kept silent?

No doubt she would say that she did not want to confront me with my grandmother's "shame." But I felt that her real reason had been a hatred of my grandmother, that secret Papist, and of my father, who perhaps had rebelled repeatedly against her iron rule in the kitchen, and who most certainly had run off to fight for another Papist. The last thing she would have wanted would be to see Sara Fraser Logan's granddaughter, Walter Logan's daughter, recognized as a Macduveen. Perhaps she had been hoping these past months that I, like my father, would flee her kitchen, and do so before someone else recognized my heritage in my face.

Alex Fraser had turned to Ian MacElvin. "If it suits you, I will go now."

Ian MacElvin nodded. "My thanks to you." I saw him dip fingers into the pocket of his silk tartan waistcoat, saw a glint of gold as he held something out to Alex Fraser.

The old man said with dignity, "No need of that, Mr. MacElvin. It is for the sake of the lass that I came here to tell the truth. It is not right that she should be so alone in the world."

He looked gravely at each person in the room, nodded, and then walked to the door.

When he had gone, leaving a silence behind him, I too looked around the room. At Clarence MacElvin, who still sat with his dark eyes fixed enigmatically on the far wall. At his proud, handsome wife, whose dilated nostrils showed how little she found the situation to her taste. At Lady Macduveen, who smiled at me, but whose dismayed brown eyes seemed to hold the wish that her late husband's young brother had broken his reckless neck before, rather than after, Sara Fraser had become the household sempstress. At the very least, I reflected, she must be wishing that Malcolm's by-blow, my father, had kept himself and his daughter on the other side of the Atlantic.

I looked at Ian MacElvin's wife. Her round face under the faded red hair was so troubled, and her blue eyes so frightened, that even before I remembered the kitchen gossip about her "daft" love for her husband, I felt a swift compassion. Was she that jealous of her husband's long-dead love? Or was she afraid that he might transfer that love to me, a girl young enough to be his granddaughter?

Last of all I looked at Donald Macduveen, still lounging against the fireplace mantel. The smile with which he returned my gaze held a covert sneer, but I could see uneasiness in his eyes. Perhaps he wondered if my circumstances might alter to the point that I could even some old scores.

Ian MacElvin said, "Elizabeth, please sit down."

When I had taken the chair he held for me, he said, still standing, "I have conferred with my wife, and with my brother and his wife, and with Lady Macduveen. We all agree that your situation cannot remain as it is. That is true, is it not, Lady Macduveen?"

"Quite true." Seeing her bright, fixed smile, I recalled hearing from more than one source that it was MacElvin money which had kept Bowain Castle from being sold for her son's debts. More specifically, it was Ian MacElvin's money. Although it was the older brother who held title to the estate adjoining the Macduveen lands, it was Ian who had become the richer, through investments in West

Indian sugar plantations and South African cattle lands. In addition to the new house he had built near the ancestral MacElvin manor, he owned an older house in Inverness, and another in London.

"And so," Ian MacElvin said, "my wife and I would like to become your guardians. Is that agreeable?"

Was there any need to ask? Certainly not of me, who only an hour before had planned to slip away from this place, ride in a creaking cart to Inverness, and there take whatever employment I could find. "Of course it is agreeable. And I am more grateful than I can express."

"Splendid. Now I must explain that my wife and I travel a great deal. In fact next week we sail for a visit to South Africa, where our second son manages our holdings. And so my wife feels, in fact we both feel, that for the present it would be best for you to remain here, with a suitable allowance from us, of course. Later on we will be delighted to have you spend as much time as possible with us."

I was silent. In Bowain Wood, Charles Edward and I had agreed that it would be folly for me to remain here. But although I did not know the identity of my enemy, I did know one thing. He or she was a coward, afraid to move openly and directly against even a penniless, friendless kitchen wench. If he had been any other sort, he long since would have come to that cobbler's hut one night and thrust a knife into my heart as I slept. Surely such a person would make no further attempt against a young woman who was an acknowledged Macduveen, and the ward of a rich and powerful man.

I said finally, "It is agreeable." I looked at the anxious-faced little woman on the sofa, trying to make my smile

139

reassuring. I wished that I could tell her that, no matter how grateful I was to her husband, he could never be the irresistible figure in my eyes that he so plainly was in hers. No, not even if he wanted to be, and I was sure he did not.

My gaze moved to the woman next to her. "Lady Macduveen, are you willing to have me here?"

Her tone was bright. "Most certainly. I have already ordered that a room be prepared for you for tonight. And tomorrow you may choose whatever room you wish to be yours from then on."

I knew which room it would be, if she really gave me my choice—Arabella's room. And I would replace the tattered hangings and canopy with silk of the same shade of yellow.

Ian MacElvin, his eyes cold now, was looking at his brother. "Are these arrangements satisfactory to you and your wife, Clarence?"

The elder MacElvin's voice was curt. "I have told you they were."

Ian flushed. He started to say something, seemed to change his mind, and then, apparently, changed it again. "But what you have not told me, at least not to my satisfaction, is why you did not tell me months ago that Elizabeth was here. True, I was in London, but you could easily have sent me word."

"But I did explain my silence on that point. The girl looked vaguely familiar, but that was all."

Ian's flush deepened. "I do not believe you. Arabella was your wife. Surely you remembered her face clearly enough to see that this girl—"

"Very well!" Clarence's face too was flushed now. "I

did see that they were almost as much alike as two peas, and that she must be of Macduveen blood. But the question was, from which Macduveen did she descend?"

He hesitated, as if half afraid to continue, and then went on even more forcibly than before, "It might have been Arabella. It would not be the first time a girl of gentle blood secretly gave birth, palmed off her illegitimate child on some low-born couple, and then married a man of her own rank. And if that had been the case here— well, a man does not like to have it known that he was cuckolded even before he was wed!"

I saw Ian MacElvin's fists clench. He took a step toward his brother and then checked himself. "Very well." His voice was thick. "I accept your explanation, although it is one that does you little credit. In fact, now that you have revealed the quality of your mind, I wonder even less that after Arabella became your wife—"

He broke off, perhaps because he feared his own rising anger, perhaps because he had remembered that his brother's present wife was in the room.

He turned back to me. "Now there is the matter of your name. I am sure that Lady Macduveen and her son would make no objection if you took the name of Macduveen." His tone, although pleasant, seemed to warn that they had better *not* object. "You are also free to take the name Mac-Elvin, if you wish."

I said, without having to think about it, "Thank you, but I was very proud of my father. I would prefer to keep his name."

He looked startled at that, and then pleased. Bending, he kissed my cheek. I think it was not until that moment that he began to think of me as a person in my own right, rather than the grandniece of his long-dead love.

Donald Macduveen was moving toward me. He said, "Since it appears that we are first cousins, may I claim the cousinly privilege?"

"First cousins once removed," I corrected evenly. "Sir James was your father. His brother Malcolm was my grandfather." He said, bending, "Nevertheless . . ." I allowed his plump lips to touch my cheek. When he straightened, we exchanged a long look. It declared a kind of truce between us. We would never be friends, his eyes and mine silently acknowledged. But on the other hand, we need not be at each other's throats.

Smiling, Ian MacElvin said to the room at large, "There is French wine down in our coach. Lady Macduveen, will you have someone fetch it?"

Rising, she pulled the bell rope. Gerald must have been hovering near the door, because only seconds passed before he shuffled in.

It was the sight of my fellow servant, I think, which made me conscious of the full enormity of what had happened to me within the last few minutes. I felt a kind of numbing awe.

Last June, on the road leading up to Castle Bowain, a few words of Kenneth's had destroyed my whole future world, a world in which my father, if he did not live, would at least die in comfort, leaving me in the protection of my kinfolk. Now, three months later, a few words from Ian MacElvin had made that world whole again.

Not in its entirety, of course. The past could not be changed. My father still had died in an abandoned cowshed, and been buried in a hillside grave. Months of hard labor had coarsened and reddened my hands, and moments of humiliation and of terror had scarred my memory. Furthermore, my father's Macduveen blood had been illegitimate, and that would count against me in the eyes of many.

Nevertheless, the wish I had harbored in childhood was coming true. For as long as I chose, I could live as a Macduveen at Bowain Castle, and look out of Arabella's window at the sloping moor, and, whenever the fancy took me, climb the stairs to one of the corner towers to watch the island of Skye change its colors in the everchanging light, like an island in a dream.

Still feeling dazed, I heard Lady Macduveen order that the wine be brought up.

Sixteen

It was in Inverness, in the summer of 1750, that I saw John Harwood again.

I stood that day at the window of the room I always occupied when staying at the MacElvins' tall old house on Inverness's High Street. Across the way the ancient Mercat cross rose from the Stone of Tubs, a platform upon which many generations of Inverness women, before toiling the rest of the way up the street, had rested the water-filled buckets they had carried up from the river. On this August afternoon a half dozen of them had gathered around the stone to chat and to ease their tired arms. As always when I saw them, I remember how my own arms used to ache when I carried water from the castle well into the kitchen. And as always, I felt renewed gratitude to the kindly pair who had rescued me from drudgery and loneliness.

Dora MacElvin—Aunt Dora to me now—had long since lost her jealous fear of me. In fact, a warm affection had sprung up between us. To me she was almost the mother I had lost as a very young girl. To her I was almost the daughter that she, the mother of three grown sons, had always wanted. I am sure she enjoyed more than I did our twice-yearly excursions to London, where we would stay at the MacElvin house in Russell Square and visit all the shops, and buy, at her insistence, more gloves and stays and dress material than I really required.

No such closeness had developed between Lady Mac-duveen and me. She remained courteous, placid, and aloof. I did not mind in the least. I had my room—Arabella's room. And I had the moors and the glens which I still roamed in almost any sort of weather, delighting in the deep purple and blue of heathery moor and distant mountains when clouds passed overhead, and then, the next moment, delighting in the sun that struck answering light almost everywhere—on the shiny, dancing leaves of poplars, on the foam of racing burns, and on mica-flecked granite rocks, so that they gleamed like patches of snow.

And I had my father's grave. The MacElvins had told me that, if I so desired, they would arrange to have his coffin reburied in the churchyard at Garlaig. I had decided against it. He had died in his own religion, and with his soul at peace. Best to leave his mortal remains undisturbed, there near the grave of the tragic young woman who, although only five years older than he, had been his aunt.

As for Donald Macduveen and me, we had kept to the tacit truce we had made that day in his mother's sitting room. Often he was away from Bowain Castle, roistering with his friends on someone else's estate or—so I gathered from the MacElvins—in Edinburgh's taverns and brothels. But whenever we were both at Castle Bowain, we treated each other with outward friendliness.

For a short time after I became Ian MacElvin's legal ward, a certain gallantry in Donald Macduveen's manner had hinted that he aspired to more than friendship. Whether he was merely amusing himself, or whether he thought my new status would make it profitable to marry me, I do not know. Whatever his motive, he desisted when he saw how little I welcomed his elaborate compliments.

To Aunt Dora's sorrow, I had also rebuffed other potential husbands. Not that any man with a title or considerable wealth had sought me out. After all, my father had been of illegitimate birth, and everyone knew it. But three eligible suitors had come my way—a younger son of a marquis, and two business associates of Ian MacElvin. I had discouraged all three of them.

To Aunt Dora, thirty years the wife of a beloved husband, my behavior seemed incomprehensible. Yes, even after I had told her about John Harwood. Did I, she asked, anxiety clouding her round face, intend to remain a spinster all my life just because of a man on whom I had once set my heart? Surely he had not been so foolish. The chances were overwhelming that by now he was not only a husband, but a father twice or three times over.

I realized that far more keenly than she ever could. There were still times when the thought of John Harwood married to some other woman, sharing his bed with her, and tossing their child in his arms, was like a knife thrust in my breast. But the realization that probably he now thought of me seldom, or not at all, made me no more inclined to marry just for the sake of enhanced social status, or even for the sake of having children. Better to live as I did now than with some man for whom I could feel

146

only tepid affection. Yes, even though there seemed little chance that I would ever see John Harwood again.

But I did see him that bright August afternoon, only about half an hour after the MacElvins had brought me from Bowain Castle to their Inverness house. Leaving a maid to finish unpacking my trunk, I had crossed to the window to look down through the white lace curtain. As I stood there, I saw two well-dressed men and a woman in a hooded, fur-trimmed cloak moving up the sidewalk. They stopped near the group of women around the Stone of Tubs and looked at the MacElvin house, as if wondering whether or not it was the one they sought. It was then that I saw that the woman was Charity Clayman, her up-turned face older and even plainer now, but still appealing in its gentleness. The elder of the two men was her father, and the other was John Harwood. His face, under his tricorn hat, was also older than the one engraved on my memory, and much more self-assured. But as I was learning, it still had the power to make me feel physically weak, as if my bones had softened. I clutched the window frame.

John said something to Mr. Clayman. The three of them started across the street. I clung to the window frame for another second or two and then, pulses racing, turned around. Halfway across the room I halted. How would I appear to John? When we last saw each other, I had been eighteen. Now I was nearing twenty-three.

I could hear voices in the ground floor hall. Careless of the maid's curious stare, I sat down at the dressing table, smoothed my hair, and gazed searchingly at my reflection. It seemed to me that my face had not changed at all. But of course it must have, in four and a half years.

And then my face began to burn with the realization of my own foolishness. Charity was with him. Charity was his wife. Why would she be here, why should she have made that long and uncomfortable journey across the ocean, if not because she found the thought of separation from her husband unendurable? Women like Charity, with mothers and sisters and brothers, did not spend weeks on a tossing ship just to be near their fathers.

No longer greatly concerned with how I looked, I rose from the dressing table and went down the stairs.

Seventeen

As I neared the drawing room, I heard several voices, including the MacElvins'. Apparently the visitors had introduced themselves. Just inside the doorway I dropped a curtsy and then, with a smile I knew was too fixed and bright, looked at Charity, at her father, and finally at John.

I said, "This is indeed a surprise. What brings all of you to Scotland?"

John was looking at me with that smile I remembered. Feeling a rush of that old longing and pain, I almost hated him for having come here. "Business has brought us," he said.

"The tobacco business," Mr. Clayman added. Now I noticed that the bushy sideburns bracketing his thin, pleasantly shrewd face, a grizzled brown when I had last seen him, were gray. "As I was telling Mr. and Mrs. MacElvin, John and I now have an interest in a Virginia tobacco plantation. We have just signed a contract with a Glasgow firm to send them two shiploads a year."

I said, still with that smile that made my mouth ache,

"Then you have given up the law, John?"

"No, nor my share of the Harwood farm, either. But farming does not take up all of a man's time, and in a small village practicing law takes even less."

I wished he had not mentioned his share of the Harwood farm, where he and I had planned to build our house overlooking the fields of Shinnecock Bay. Why had he come here, anyway? To torment me? No, of course not. Surely it was just that he had thought the memory of our love would have grown as dim for me as it had for him, so that to me he and Charity would be merely old friends from across the ocean.

"As I was telling Mr. Clayman and Mr. Harwood before you came in," my guardian said, "it might be wise for one of them to stay here permanently." As always when he spoke of financial matters, his face and his voice were animated. "The tobacco business is brisk in Scotland— very brisk indeed. You might find daily association with our merchants very profitable."

"We have discussed my becoming the firm's representative in Scotland," John said.

My heart cried out in silent protest. It was painful enough that they had come here. Would I, now, be expected to stand as godmother to their children?

Since I knew I must exchange courtesies with her sooner or later, I turned to Charity. "How pleasant that you could come to Scotland too." I added, with bright falsity, "It is good to see you. You are looking very well."

The wryness in her large brown eyes, her best feature, told me that she knew the years had not improved her looks. "Thank you, Elizabeth."

"And your mother and your brother and sisters? How are they?"

"My brother and both my sisters are married now." She paused, and then added quietly, "My mother died last March."

"Oh, I am so sorry." And I was. I had liked Mrs. Clayman, a handsome, friendly woman who, unfortunately, had passed her good looks on to her son rather than to any of her daughters. But at the same time I felt a selfish surge of hope. Perhaps it was because Charity and her father were now alone that she had undertaken the long voyage.

Aunt Dora said, "Elizabeth." I turned to her. From the bright urgency in her face I knew that she had been trying to catch my eye ever since I entered the room. "Can't you persuade Miss Clayman and her father to stay with us? Surely they cannot be very comfortable at the inn."

A weight seemed to lift from my chest, so that once more I could breathe normally. I warned myself, though, not to hope too much or too quickly. Charity was far from being the only girl he might have married.

"Thank you, Mrs. MacElvin," her father was saying, "but representatives of various shipping firms will be calling upon us at the inn. We decided that since we were to be in Inverness anyway, we might as well learn if some company here could offer us better rates than American and Glasgow shippers have."

A serving man had come in, carrying a tray laden with wineglasses. The conversation became general then. From it I learned that John and the Claymans had gone by hired coach from Glasgow to Bowain Castle. There Lady Macduveen had told them that I had gone to Inverness with the MacElvins. When I heard that, I felt there was no longer any need to restrain my hope. Business matters might have brought John to Glasgow. It was I who had brought him to the north.

"Lady Macduveen told us about your father." The restraint in Mr. Clayman's voice reminded me that he, like every other man in Southampton, had voted to banish Walter Logan. "We were sorry to hear of his death."

What else had she told him? That my father had died in a cowshed? That I myself for four months had drudged in the castle kitchen? No, it would have been unpleasant to tell them that, and Lady Macduveen avoided unpleasantness whenever possible.

I turned to John and added, trying to make my voice light, "I am surprised you remembered the name of my father's birthplace. I cannot recall mentioning Bowain Castle to you more than a few times."

John said quietly, "I remembered."

Aunt Dora broke the brief silence. "Have you seen the view from the bridge at the foot of this street, Mr. Harwood? It is considered very fine, especially toward evening."

"No, I have not, Mrs. MacElvin."

"Elizabeth, why don't you show it to him? You've had no exercise today. A turn in the fresh air would do you good."

I felt color in my face. Concealment of her emotions or her motives had never been Dora MacElvin's strong point. I said, "If John wants to see the view—"

"I do."

"Then if everyone will excuse me, I will get my cloak."

As I rose, I saw Charity looking at John with defeated

longing in her brown eyes. I knew then that it was not just to be with her bereaved father that she had crossed the ocean. She must have been hoping that John would not find me, or would find me married. I felt a moment's sharp compassion for her. But as I hurried up the stairs, all thought of her was drowned by my eagerness to be out on the windy high street with John.

Eighteen

Even on a bright afternoon in August, Inverness air can be brisk. As we moved down the sloping high street, past the tall houses with their ground floor shops, past the ruins of the castle, blown up by my barefooted friend Charles Edward during the months when he was moving from victory to victory in northern Scotland, past the large house where his ancestress, Mary Queen of Scots, had lodged when her Scottish enemies had denied her entrance to that same castle, a sharp wind tore at my green velvet cloak and plucked strands of hair from beneath my hood to blow across my face.

For a while we walked in silence. Then, because I could no longer wait to make sure, absolutely sure, I asked, "John, do you have a wife?"

"No. And you, are you pledged to anyone?"

The sharpness of his tone told me that, beneath that controlled manner of his, he had been as anxious as I. "No."

My heart swelled with exultation. He still loved me. He had followed me to this tumultuous but beautiful land,

and here we would marry. Surely some such thought, such hope, had been in his mind when he came here. He could manage the Scottish affairs of the tobacco firm. Perhaps he could even be admitted to the practice of law in Scotland. And he and I would live an ocean away from that Long Island village and the bitter memories it held for both of us.

What had become of my bitterness toward him? When had it departed from me, leaving only my stubborn love for him? Perhaps I had buried it there in the dawn light that day I had buried my father. I could not be sure. All I knew was that now I accepted what John had done. He would not have been the strong, disciplined man I loved if, after taking his oath to uphold the law, he had not found my father guilty of the charges our village had brought against him.

He said, "When Lady Macduveen mentioned that she had a son, I thought perhaps—"

"That I might be pledged to him?" I laughed. "It is hard to imagine any woman wanting to marry Donald Macduveen."

"But surely it has not been for lack of suitors that you are still free." Emotion had roughened his voice. "You seem to me lovelier than before, and I do not think it is just because of your fine clothes."

I savored that for a long moment. Then I thought, "Best to tell him now." I was almost sure it would make no difference to him. But still, best to tell him.

We were midway of the stone bridge's span now. I halted and looked up at him. "Yes, I have had a few suitors, but none to my liking, and none as rich or well-placed as you might think. You see, John, my father was the son of a younger brother of a baronet. But he was not a legitimate son. That makes a difference."

I saw surprise in his face, and puzzlement, but nothing that resembled shock. Then he must have read at least some anxiety in my eyes, because he said, "It does not make a difference, not to me. But I think you had best tell me all about it."

As we leaned against the bridge parapet, looking down the wind-ruffled river toward the bluff guarding the entrance to Moray Firth, I did tell him. The bitter journey north. My father's death, and his burial near that other lonely grave. Those months which had brought me, not only the hardest sort of toil, but moments of terror too. "That pistol shot into the courtyard and my plunge down those stairs both could have been accidents. But that note, of course, was quite another matter."

John's face had grown pale. "Who could have done that to you, a helpless young girl? Who could have *wanted* to?"

"I still do not know." Many times during the past four years I had pondered that question. Either of the Macduveens could have forged that note and slipped it under my door during the night. So could Clarence MacElvin or his wife. The MacElvin manor house was only eight miles from Bowain Castle. For that matter—although the idea was too absurd to entertain for even a moment—my kind, business-absorbed guardian or his wife, my loving Aunt Dora, could have sent me into that bog. They had been staying at their own house on the family lands that September of four years ago.

And any one of several of the servants could have written the note. I managed to find that out, the first week after my status changed from kitchen wench to family member, by asking seemingly casual questions of Lady Macduveen. The aged footman and two equally aged serving women she had brought with her to Bowain Castle were all illiterate. But Jenny and Mag and Kenneth and Angus, each the offspring of stern Covenanter parents, had learned their letters in childhood.

As for Murdock, I had been unable to learn whether or not the mute falcon keeper could read and write. Probably he had never learned, or, if he had learned in his long-ago childhood, had forgotten during his many years of silence and isolation. It was an isolation I had not again attempted to invade. Absurd as his threat had been that day, I had been a little frightened by his wild aspect, and more than a little repelled by the odor of aged flesh and long unwashed clothing.

John said, "How could you have stayed on there?"

"I had not planned to. I had planned to slip away, first to Garlaig, then to Inverness, and find work there." I told him of the button Charles Edward had wrenched from his ragged coat and given to me, together with instructions to show it to the carter in Garlaig.

"But within a few minutes after I returned to the castle that day, my whole world had changed. I was no longer a penniless servant with no one to care whether she lived or died. My father *had* been a Macduveen, even though from the wrong side of the blanket."

He was frowning. "And that made you feel safe?"

"Safe enough to take what was offered, instead of slaving in someone's kitchen in Inverness! And I was right. There have been no more tricks played on me, not once in the past four years."

It was in part my reading of my enemy's character

157

which made me feel safe. Whoever he—or she—was, he was more than cowardly. His was one of those self-divided natures, chronically given to half measures. Instead of attacking swiftly and decisively some night as I lay asleep in the cobbler's hut, what had he done? He had—perhaps—fired at me at night in the courtyard, when chances were excellent that he might miss. He had—perhaps—pushed me down the turret stairs, with no surety that the plunge would be fatal. And he had directed my steps into the bog, without being absolutely certain that no one would hear my screams, as indeed someone had.

A person so lacking in cold-blooded resolve as to bungle the death of a friendless servant, I felt, would certainly make no move to attack Ian MacElvin's ward. And so it had proved to be.

"You say this Stuart fellow gave you a button from his coat?"

Hearing the jealousy in his voice, I smiled inwardly. "Yes." And a kiss, too. But I would never tell John about that.

"They say he is handsome."

"Yes, and brave. But—"

"But what?"

"Many who worship him would not agree, but I would say it is plain now that it was an evil day for Scotland when he raised his banner in the Highlands."

Less than a week after I had sat shivering beside his fire in Bowain Wood, Charles had shipped aboard a French ship and sailed away. His physical ordeal was over. But Scotland's ordeal remained. True, the dungeons in the Tolbooth cellar here in Inverness and the stinking prison ships anchored in London's Thames River had long since delivered up their wretched inmates—a few to freedom, many to death by disease or on the gallows, many others to the transports carrying bondservants to America and the West Indies. But Scotland's punishment was not ended. Possession of a claymore, the fearsome Highland broadsword, was punishable by death. Bewildered crofters, who had lived all their lives by raising cattle, had been dragged from their lonely glens, hurried to coastal villages, and told that if they did not want to starve they must learn the skills of fishermen or weavers. What seemed to me most humiliating of all was a comparatively minor stricture. Highland dress, including the bonnet, plaid, and kilt, was strictly forbidden. All Scotsmen must wear trousers, even if they were too poor to buy new cloth to make them. And so in the villages and on the roads and even here in Inverness, you saw them by the hundreds— once proud Highlanders in pitiful, ridiculous-looking breeches they had made by sewing a central seam in their faded kilts.

As for the Prince, he was said to be moving with a small entourage from one European capital to another, trying to gain support for another landing in Scotland. It was also said that his liking for strong drink, understandable enough when he was an often cold and hungry fugitive, had not diminished now that he lived in safety.

I said, "I don't think there will ever be another Stuart rising."

"And what should that matter to us? Why should we be concerned with Charles Stuart or his father? Elizabeth, look at me!"

Heartbeats quickening, I looked up at him. He said,

"Do you know why I have not married?"

After four years of longing for this man, I felt little inclined toward maidenly coyness. "I think so. I think it is for the same reason that I have not."

I saw the leap of joy in his eyes. "Then you will marry me?"

"Yes, John. Yes!"

From the way his gaze went over my face, lingering on my mouth, I knew he wanted to catch me in his arms and kiss me, just as I longed for him too. But it was still broad daylight. And although no one was crossing the bridge at the moment, people moved along both embankments. Later there would be time for kisses—all the time we chose to take.

"Will you marry me right away? We have four lost years to make up for."

"Of course I will."

"Then we will marry before we sail. I suppose you would rather be married in your guardian's house anyway. I could see that the three of you are fond of each other."

The brisk breeze, until now only exhilarating, felt suddenly cold. "Sail? Sail where?"

"Why, home, of course. Southampton."

"Southampton is not my home!" I said wildly. "Scotland is. And I thought you were ready to make it your home."

"Whatever gave—"

"When Ian MacElvin suggested it might be best for you to remain in Scotland, you said you and Mr. Clayman had considered it."

"Considered it, yes, and decided against it."

"Why didn't you say so, right then?" I felt a foreboding, almost a despair. Were our wills always to clash, with both of us the loser?

"Because Mr. MacElvin is an older man, and your guardian. I did not want to argue with him. And it might be wise to have someone stationed permanently in Scotland. Perhaps, if the business grows, we will send someone. But it will not be me. My great-grandfather helped found Southampton Colony. The house where I was born is there. My law practice is there. All my roots are in Southampton, Elizabeth, and so are yours."

"If they were, the people there tore them up! They stripped my father of everything—his pupils, his house, everything, and then turned him out to die."

John's face looked bleak. "I too voted to banish him."

"Yes! But I can forgive you because I know how loath you were to do it. You voted out of principle, not as many of the others did, because they resented his clothes and his manners or his learning, or wanted his house! I cannot get over my bitterness toward them; I cannot."

After a moment he said quietly, "Not even for the sake of love?"

I looked at him with desperate need. Then, in my mind's eye, I saw myself moving along Southampton's streets, coming face to face with men who had exiled my father, and with their wives who, aware that we could not refuse their offers, had bought our household goods at a fraction of their worth.

"I cannot live surrounded by people I so detest. I would be unhappy, and I would make you unhappy. And we could both be so happy here. Scotland is a lovely place. And my guardian is rich. If you needed money to expand your business—"

"No, Elizabeth. Southampton is my home. I will live

there, and so will my wife, and my children will grow up there."

As we gazed at each other, I knew my face must appear as wretched as his. "I love you, Elizabeth. For four years, loving you has kept me from turning to another woman. But I will be thirty my next birthday. It is time I had a wife, a home, and sons."

He paused for a moment, and then went on evenly, "It is you I want to marry. I know it would not be easy for you at first, living in that village. But time has a way of softening everything, even bitterness. And surely our happiness in our home should compensate you for whatever unhappy memories your surroundings awake in you."

I looked at him in silent misery. How could he be so cruel? How could he force me to choose between parting from him again, or living with him among people who had so grievously injured my father and me?

"When you turned away from me four years ago, Elizabeth, I came back three times in hope that I could induce you to change your mind. This time you will have to come to me. We will be staying at the inn until Friday. Then we will leave for Glasgow. Whether or not I will ever again be in Scotland, I cannot say."

Friday. Four days from now. If he had loved me enough to remain unmarried for four years, surely four days would be sufficient for him to realize his unreasonableness. Surely he would see that, aside from any consideration of my happiness, it would be to his financial advantage to stay in Scotland, befriended by a man many times richer than the richest man in Southampton.

I said, from a tight throat, "It is getting late. We had best go back."

In silence we moved up High Street through the fading light, and entered the house. The others were still in the drawing room. At sight of our faces, dismay leaped into Aunt Dora's eyes. She said, in a falsely bright voice, "I am glad you are back. Supper will be served soon."

"I am sorry, Mrs. MacElvin," John said, "but we have an engagement at the inn." He looked at his partner. "Had you forgotten that a representative of the Caledonian Shipping Company was to have supper with us?"

Mr. Clayman looked puzzled for a moment, and then said, in an embarrassed voice, "Why, yes. I had forgotten."

I felt tears of pain and anger pressing behind my eyes. Dropping a curtsy to Aunt Dora, I said, "Will you excuse me, ma'am? I am not feeling well."

I left the drawing room, crossed the hall, and, clutching my skirts with both hands, fled up the stairs.

Nineteen

Around ten o'clock that night Aunt Dora sat beside my bed wringing out a handkerchief dipped in cold water to place it on my tear-swollen eyes.

"Such a foolish young man," she said. "Here in Scotland my husband could help him to become rich before he is thirty-five. Why should he insist upon returning to that raw little colony set down in the wilderness, especially when you detest it so?"

I could hear the mixture of emotion in her voice. My distress had awakened her pain and indignation. But at the same time she could not help feeling glad that I had refused to return to America. She said, "Surely he will realize his own foolishness."

"Perhaps. But he is very strong-willed." I realized that some might say that of me. But I had common sense on my side.

"Don't fret, my pretty. He loves you. Why else should a handsome and able man have remained unmarried? Once he realizes that he cannot carry you back across the ocean with him, he will stay on this side of it. Can you sleep now? Do try."

When she had left me, I did not sleep. I rose, put a robe on over my nightdress, and carried the lighted taper from my bedside table to the rosewood writing desk in one corner of the room. From one of the little drawers I took Arabella's diary, a small volume bound in frayed red silk. Despite my aching eyes, I wanted to read her words. I needed them to remind me of wind keening through heather, of Skye's mountains golden in sunset light, of all that John asked me to leave in favor of a village where every face would bring the taste of gall to my mouth.

Even before I had ever opened her diary or any of her much-underlined books, I had begun to feel an almost mystical bond with my dead ancestress. Sleeping in the bed that had been hers, looking into the mirror that must have reflected often her so-similar face, gazing from the window at the sloping moor, purple with heather and green or brown with bracken, which so often must have delighted her eyes, I began to feel that it was not just I who dwelt in that room. At times it was almost as if she were there too, living again through me, touching the yellow brocade bed hangings with my fingers and drinking in the printed lines with my eyes.

It was when I began to read the books on the wall shelf beside the bed—books unnoticed by me that first time I had slipped into her room—that my sense of closeness to Arabella increased. To judge by her portrait she might have been some feather-brained young aristocrat, unconcerned with anything but her face and the latest London fashions. Instead she had not only owned books—Chaucer, Herrick, Shakespeare, Dryden, Donne—but had read them. Many passages were underlined. In the small, neat hand that was to become familiar to me through her diary, she had written brief comments in the margins—"I have not found it so," or "How wise!" or once, beside one of Milton's dissertations on the feebleness of female intellect, the single word "Bosh!"

But it was her diary that made my great-aunt so real to me that sometimes I found it hard to realize that we had not been contemporaries and friends, that I had not actually shared with her all the emotions she had felt in this room—delight, and longing for a beloved, and rebellion and bitter hatred.

It was old Angus who had found the diary and handed it to me one day when he replaced a cracked board in the window seat. The small book, its silken cover split and mildewed, had been wedged in a narrow space between the wall and the window seat's frame. Now, even as I had that morning in Bowain Castle, I opened the book and began to read.

The first page had been dated Fifth of September, 1707. The entry read: "My brother James returned from London today. He brought me not only this journal and the poems of Robert Herrick, which I had asked for, but a doll! Does he not know that I am twelve years old? Perhaps not. I wish James was not so much taken up with being a laird, and not so much older than me. Almost twenty years! I wish my brother Malcolm had chosen some other mount to ride that day. I was only five when he was killed, but I can remember how much younger he seemed than James, and lighter of heart."

As always when I read those words, I felt an even stronger sense of kinship with Arabella. Malcolm, her twenty-year-old brother who had seduced the castle sempstress and then been thrown to his death by an unruly horse. Had he known that the sempstress was to give birth to his child? Probably not.

I wondered too how often the young girl Arabella had looked down into the castle courtyard and seen her brother's son, a boy only five years younger than herself, hurrying about his tasks under Jenny's harsh direction. No matter how often she had observed young Walter Logan, it was unlikely indeed that she had ever guessed that the castle potboy was her nephew.

That first entry in her diary continued: "How pleased I am with Robert Herrick! He loved all the things that I love—Christmas and Morris Dancers, and birds—even hens!—and flowers, and strawberries, and early mornings. And he was so merry. To think he was a churchman! I wish our clergymen were more like that. But that is a wicked thing to say. Herrick must have been tainted with Popery. Why else should the Puritan soldiers have turned him out of his church? And I, like our sovereign, Queen Anne, am a loyal Protestant and abhor all Papists.

"On the moor today I saw an eagle soaring. It gave me a dizzy but delightful feeling, as if it were I up there, beating the air with my wings. And beside a burn I found three stalks of butterfly flowers. I know they are called heath orchids, but I have my own names for things."

I too, kneeling beside a heath orchid, had been reminded of lavender butterflies with brown-freckled wings.

She had not written every day, or even every week. Perhaps she had been too busy living. But when she had turned to her diary, it usually had been to write of her books, or of one of the ever-changing aspects—green bracken giving way to brown, golden broom to bluebells and maiden pinks—of the moors. Apparently, like me, she had wandered outdoors in all sorts of weather. An entry written in her fourteenth year told me that James's wife, the first Lady Macduveen, had "berated" her when she returned to the castle "rain-soaked to my pelt."

As she grew older, her literary enthusiasms, as recorded in her diary, had changed. By the time she was seventeen she had esteemed Herrick much less than before, and Shakespeare and Dryden much more. Too, she had begun to copy lines of poetry in her diary, perhaps as an aid to memorizing them. Her political and religious opinions, in the beginning no more than an echo of the adults around her, began to seem heartfelt convictions of her own. She disliked the Tories ("secret Papists, all of them!"), and esteemed Queen Anne's Whig minister. She mourned Queen Anne's sorrows—"nine times brought to bed, and no living child"—and feared that after Anne's death the exiled Stuarts would try to seize the throne "and deliver us into the Pope's hands."

But neither politics nor poetry had replaced her delight in the wild, jumbled landscape stretching around her. Almost every entry spoke of a rare flower discovered in some narrow glen, or graylag geese dark against the sky, or a herd of shaggy red Highland deer thundering away across the heather at her approach.

In the early spring of 1714, in her eighteenth year, she had traveled with her brother James and his wife to be presented at court. It must have been shortly before Queen Anne's death. ("She appears monstrous fat, poor lady. But it is not gluttony. She is dropsical.") Clarence and Ian MacElvin were in London at the same time, and the three young people went riding together. It was there, in Hyde Park, that she fell in love with Ian.

"I wore my new blue velvet riding habit." I felt I could see her in it, her knee under the flowing skirt hooked around the horn of the side saddle, her face, under her plumed hat, flushed with the excitement of being in London, and with Ian. "Clarence's horse was strong-mouthed, and kept bolting ahead of Ian's mount and mine, leaving us alone. This pleased me greatly. I do not like Clarence, even though he is already a Whig leader in Scotland, and a well-known supporter of the Protestant succession. His face is too long. And when he thinks I do not see, he has a way of looking at me that makes me feel naked.

"It is Ian that I favor. I think I always have, even when we were much younger. He is so handsome, and his eyes are so brown and warm, and his mouth— I find myself wondering what it would be like to have his mouth touch my own."

It was hard for me to imagine my kind, brisk, business-absorbed guardian, a grandfather several times over, as the romantic figure Arabella described. But, of course, he must have been in his early twenties then.

Several days later, still in London, she had written: "I have been to four balls, and the MacElvin brothers were in attendance at three of them. I love Ian. And he loves me. In every way but with words he has told me so—with his eyes, the tone of his voice, the pressure of his hand when we meet in the figures of the dance.

"Clarence's hands are cold and clammy."

I had meant to stop reading there. I knew there were no more references in her diary to birdsong and the smell of sun-warmed heather. And no joy. But when I closed the book, I instantly saw John's bleak, set face looking down at me as he said, "This time you will have to come to me."

I reopened the diary and went on reading.

A month later, back in Scotland, she had written: "My brother summoned me to him today. Clarence MacElvin was there. James left me alone with Clarence. He asked me to marry him, and I refused. Afterward I had a terrible quarrel with James. I told him that I loved Ian. He said that Ian has not the influence at court of his brother, nor the land, nor the money. All that is true, although Ian has told me that he intends to become very rich. But whether he does or not does not matter. I love him, I love him."

The writing had become ragged. Evidently she had laid down the pen until she became calmer, because the next paragraph was written with her usual neatness.

"James says that if I dare to run away with Ian, it is not only I who will be disinherited. Ian's father will disinherit him, and will work with both Clarence and James to block Ian in whatever endeavor he pursues.

"I know how much Ian loves me. He told me before I left London. But I do not want to ruin him. If I cannot marry him, though, I will never marry Clarence. Never!"

For a whole year after that there were only scattered entries, some of them nothing but a few lines of poetry. I knew it had been a momentous year in the world at large. Queen Anne had died, and a German-speaking Hanoverian, George the First, had been anointed King of England, Scotland, and Ireland. The exiled Stuart pretender, the father of my ragged friend Charles Edward, had landed in Scotland and tried to rally sufficient forces to take the throne. In the Battle of Preston, which had meant

170

the death of his immediate hopes, an obscure participant had been a boy named Walter Logan.

But no word of battles appeared in Arabella's diary. The first entry after her quarrel with her brother read, "Neither James nor my sister-in-law have spoken to me for three weeks. I take all my meals in my room." The next, written after an interval of several weeks, said, "I cannot eat. I know I am alarmingly thin, but after a few mouthfuls, I have no appetite." Weeks after that she had written, "Ian smuggled a note to me this morning by one of the servants. I met him out on the moor, by the old round tower. He implored me to run away with him. I cannot. Now he thinks he could face poverty and failure for my sake, but in time he might hate me for it. Or perhaps it is just that I have lost courage, as well as flesh from my bones."

For a while after that there were only scraps of poetry, most of them by John Donne. Not Donne the Dean of St. Paul's, with his appeals to his stern God. These were lines he had written during his physically passionate younger years, when denied the woman he loved. Arabella had written a half-dozen lines of one poem, beginning with: "For God's sake, hold your tongue and let me love!" and ending with, "What merchant's ships have my sighs drowned? Who says my tears have overflowed his ground?"

Still later she had written, "I met Ian on the moor again today. It was raining. He is going to the West Indies on a business venture. He asked me to come with him. It was agony, but I refused. Is it just for his sake that I refuse? Or is it just that I, gently bred, cannot face the thought of mean lodgings, coarse food, and shabby garments? I am so tired and confused that I no longer know even my own mind."

A few days later she must have been thinking of that meeting on the rainy moor when she wrote:

> Bitter the taste of our final kiss,
> And bitter the taste of the rain,
> But would I were climbing the hill tonight
> To be in your arms again.

It was like one last, despairing cry. There were no more entries until several months later, when she wrote, "I am going to marry Clarence MacElvin. With Ian gone, I cannot hold out any longer against James and his wife and Clarence's father and Clarence himself. And if I cannot have Ian, it matters little what happens to me."

The next entry, written almost a month later, read, "My husband has gone to London, to collect rewards due him as a supporter of the new King at the time of the Stuart Rising. He expects a title as well as lands formerly owned by one of the attainted Tory lords, and I heartily hope he gets neither, although I suppose he is certain to receive some land. I have come home to stay during his absence, as I shall do at every opportunity.

"How I hate him. Dear God, how I hate my husband. What a terrible thing it is to have a woman's body, and be induced to surrender it into the hands of a man like Clarence MacElvin."

Evidently she had found even her books insufficient distraction from unhappiness, because after that bitter entry she had begun to record various efforts on behalf of the poor and sick in Garlaig and in the crofters' huts. During that stay at Bowain Castle, and a second one a few weeks later, she had written of taking wine and fruit to an old woman with a "monstrous wen" in the village, and to Murdock's stepdaughter, a "poor, motherless girl with hair as lusterless as dried straw and with black hollows under her eyes," and to Kenneth's parents, both mortally ill, and both worried about the future of their small son. Arabella had given them her brother James's assurance that Kenneth would be trained as a coachman. She had also given another crofter's widow money "to pay for a proper coffin," and distributed clothing she had worn in her own not-too-distant childhood to several village families.

In all those comings and goings she must have observed cloud shadows, and heard grouse thrumming, and seen wind tear the foam of waterfalls to ragged lace, but she made no mention of them. Perhaps such things had lost their power to move her.

The diary's last item, dated Third of June, 1716, was so bitterly triumphant, and so puzzling, that even though I knew it almost by heart, I frowned as I read it. She had written, "Clarence has gone to London, and so now I am back here, and able to write down what has happened.

"Yesterday morning a Monsieur LeClerc called at the manor house. Clarence looked so alarmed when the footman came into the drawing room to announce the visitor that I was sure the visit boded ill for him. I went upstairs, and then slipped down to listen through the closed doors.

"And now I have him, I have him! I have had to submit to him in silence in all that pertains to a wife. But in this matter silence on my part would render me as guilty as he is.

"I am afraid the footman saw me turn away from the drawing room door and go back upstairs. Perhaps he has told my husband. But I think not, since Clarence set out for London that afternoon to spend several weeks, just as he had intended to do before his visitor arrived. And anyway, nothing or no one will stop me. Since it would be folly to trust what I know to the post, just as it would be to write it in these pages, I will accompany my brother when he goes to London next week."

But she had not gone to London. According to Ian Mac-Elvin, late the next afternoon she had left the castle, telling her brother and sister-in-law that she intended to visit some of the sick she had been befriending. On June 20th, her body was washed up on the shore of the loch, still in the clothing she had worn when she left the castle. The doctor who examined her body said that she had been dead, and in the water, for at least a week. Where she had been wandering for the eight-to-ten-day interval before she drowned herself, no one ever found out. No one in the village had seen her during that time, nor any of the crofters she had previously visited.

Of course, in the light of that exultantly vindictive entry in her diary, I felt that perhaps she had not gone willingly to her death in that loch. That was why, even though I knew it would awaken painful memories, I had taken the diary one day to my guardian, in the library of the MacElvins' London house. As he read it, this grandfather and businessman who had once ridden beside a radiant Arabella Macduveen in Hyde Park, I watched the changing emotions of his face—amused tenderness, and pain, and an old, unassuaged bitterness.

When he closed the little book, I asked, "Did you know that she had discovered something reprehensible about your brother? Or, at least, thought that she had."

"No, I did not."

"Do you have any idea what it could have been?"

"No, and you can be sure he would not tell me, especially not at this late date. And if I showed him the diary—which I will not, because I could not bear for his hands to touch it—he would say that she had been mad when she wrote those words about him, and had proved her madness soon thereafter by taking her own life."

He paused and then said, "I can see that you believe someone might have drowned her in the loch. So did I. But if someone killed her, it was not Clarence. When I returned from the West Indies, soon after her body was recovered from the loch, I satisfied myself on that point. Even if her body had been in the loch two weeks instead of one, Clarence could not have put her there. For nearly a month previously he had been in London, seen each day by dozens of people at St. James or in Parliament or at his solicitor's in the Inns of Court."

We were both silent for a moment. Then he said reluctantly, "I suppose you would like to keep her diary."

"Yes. But if you—"

"No. She was your great-aunt. And I have something you do not—actual memories of her." He paused. "Promise you will not show the diary to Dora, or even tell her of its existence."

"Of course I promise." For Aunt Dora, already jealous of her husband's long-dead love, the thought of Ian and Arabella locked in each other's arms there on the rainy moor would be excruciating.

And so the matter had rested. The cruelty and degradation which had turned Arabella from a blithe young girl into a vengeful, perhaps half-mad wife I could imagine, at least dimly. But why she had sought death in the cold, deep water of the loch, or had death thrust upon her there, were questions whose answers I had little hope of learning.

I placed the frayed little book in its drawer, blew out the candle, and returned to bed. But I still could not sleep. My mind was too full of its tormenting dilemma. Now that John had come back to me, I could not bear to part with him. And yet what happiness could I know with him, or he with me, surrounded by people whose very memory filled me with bitterness?

Surely he would see that. Surely tomorrow morning I would hear the knocker strike, and then his deep voice speaking in the ground floor hall.

Twenty

But I did not, neither the next day, nor on the three days thereafter. I stayed indoors all that time. "Inverness is a small place," Aunt Dora reminded me. "If you go out, you are almost sure to encounter him. He will think you wanted the meeting, and that your resolution is weakening. That will only increase his foolish stubbornness. Make him realize that he must meet your terms or else lose you again."

They were endless, those first three days. I found sleeping difficult, eating more so, and reading impossible. On the morning of the fourth day, I awoke with renewed hope. This was his last day in Inverness. Surely he would not let it pass without walking the few hundred yards which separated the inn on Bank Street from the MacElvin house.

I spent most of the morning near my window, watching through the curtain for the first sight of his tall figure striding up High Street. With no appetite, I did not go downstairs for the midday meal.

One o'clock passed. Two. When the clock downstairs

began to strike three, my resolution crumbled. Panic washed over me. He was not coming. If I did not go to him at once, almost certainly I would lose him forever. I snatched my cloak from the wardrobe, flung it around me, and went swiftly down the stairs.

Aunt Dora was in the lower hall. "Are you going to the inn?"

"Yes."

Her face had been showing the strain of these past few days. Now her eyes were almost as frightened for me as I was for myself. She said, "You had best do that."

Afternoon sun lay warm on the sidewalk. I hurried down the slope to the river, almost as smooth as blue glass on this windless day. I passed the bakeshop and the chandler's shop. Next was the inn, its doors opened wide to the mild air. I went into the big common room and saw the fat proprietor hurrying toward me through the ale-smelling dimness. He said, "Good afternoon."

"Good afternoon. Will you please send word to Mr. Harwood that Miss Logan would like to speak to him?"

"Mr. John Harwood? He and the lady and the older gentleman left more than an hour ago for Glasgow." Then, as I reached out to clutch a chair back: "What is it? Are you ill? Sit down, and I will bring you a glass."

I managed to say, "No. It was just that it was so very important—"

"No need for despair." His face had become both sympathetic and knowing. "Glasgow is not the end of the world. And Mr. Harwood mentioned that they will be there a fortnight, staying at the Duke of Argyle, before they could sail for America."

I drew a deep breath. Should I go to Glasgow? No, not

even John would want me to do such an unwomanly thing as travel more than a hundred miles to throw myself in his arms. But two weeks would be ample time for him to receive my letter and to send a reply—or, what was much more likely, to come hurrying back to Inverness.

Aunt Dora was waiting just inside the door when I reached the house. I said, "They have gone." As she lost color, I added, "It is all right. They will be staying at a Glasgow inn for a fortnight. I can write to him."

By the next day's post, I sent the letter. It was a complete capitulation. I wrote that I would always love him, that I would live in Southampton or anyplace else he chose, and that I would strive to do so cheerfully, betraying no bitterness to our neighbors over their treatment of my father, and praying that in time all bitterness would vanish from my heart.

The next few days were happy, busy ones. Out of contrition for her part in my near disaster, as well as out of love for me, Aunt Dora summoned three sempstresses and set them to work on a trousseau—sheets, pillowcases, nightdresses, and shifts of such finely woven linen and silk that I knew they would be an embarrassment to me in that homespun Long Island village. For his part, Ian MacElvin told me that he had placed five thousand pounds to my credit in the Inverness bank. "Legally, of course, any property of yours will become your husband's. But John Harwood did not strike me as the sort of man who would spend his wife's money without her consent."

When five days had passed, I began to hope that at any moment John would appear at our door. And even if he had been unable to leave Glasgow immediately, I told myself, he would have sent a letter by now.

On the eighth day the letter arrived. I hurried up to my room with it, closed the door, and sank into a chair. With shaking fingers I tore open the envelope and folded the single sheet of paper inside. He had written:

"The captain of the ship upon which we reserved passage has readied his cargo sooner than expected. When you receive this letter, we will be at sea.

"By the time I received your letter, Elizabeth, it was already too late. During the journey from Inverness to Glasgow, I asked Charity to be my wife. The captain will marry us soon after we sail. I must do this. You know that I must. I could not break my troth with any woman, once I had made it, let alone a good and gentle woman like Charity.

"Oh, Elizabeth, my foolish darling! I warned you, I warned you. Why were you so strong-headed? And once you had embarked upon strong-headedness, why did you turn back and write that letter to me? I have destroyed it, lest by some chance Charity see it. But every word of it will remain in my memory. That letter will make it all the harder to achieve the modest contentment I had hoped to find with Charity.

"If there were any way, any way at all, for me to be with you now, I would be. You know that. And you know that I wish you well. There is nothing more for me to say."

I do not know how much time passed before Aunt Dora knocked at my door. Receiving no answer, she came in and looked at me as I sat there, John's letter still in my hand.

She said, her eyes appalled, "Oh, Elizabeth!"

Unable to speak, I handed her the letter. When she had

finished reading it, she laid it on the dressing table and said, "It is my fault. If I had not advised you—"

"No." I roused myself. "Even if you had not so advised me, I would have tested his will against mine. I would have done so, not out of sheer stubbornness, but because I believed common sense was on my side." But common sense, I reflected, might prove a cold bedfellow in the years to come.

After several seconds she said, "What do you want to do?"

"I would rather not stay here for the present." Not here, where for several days now I had been expecting to see him coming up the street, when all the time a ship was carrying him and his wife farther and farther across the Atlantic.

"Do you want to return to Bowain Castle, then?"

I shook my head. Instinctively I knew that right then the beauty of mountain and sea and moorland would seem a mockery of my pain. "Perhaps London . . ."

She began to twist her hands together. "I don't know what to do. You cannot stay in the London house with no one but servants there. And Ian and I must go to Trinidad to be with Martha soon."

Martha was the too-delicate wife of the MacElvins' eldest and favorite son. Married for twelve years, she would soon, if all went well, present her husband with their first child, and the Ian MacElvins with their sixth grandchild.

Her face brightened somewhat. "I know! There is Cousin Gertrude. She could chaperon you." Aunt Dora's distant cousin, Gertrude MacKay, was an aged and impoverished widow who lived in a small Inverness house owned by Ian MacElvin. She also, I suspected, lived chiefly off Ian's bounty.

"Very well."

"Oh, Elizabeth!" She took a step toward me.

"Please," I said. "Please don't." I felt that if she put her arms around me, I would start weeping and be unable to stop.

She said, "As you wish, dear," and left me.

Soon after the clock struck ten that night, I descended the stairs. (At its own last striking, how many bells had that ship's clock sounded? Surely the ship was still close enough to Europe that it sailed through darkness. Had John and Charity gone to their cabin?) As I entered the library, my guardian laid his book aside and rose to his feet.

I said, "Since I am not to be married, I would like for you to take back your gift of five thousand pounds."

He kissed my cheek. "No, Elizabeth. You are a mature woman now. I believe a woman should have some money of her own."

Especially a woman who seemed likely to live out her life as a spinster. He did not say that, but I could see the sad thought in his eyes.

Twenty-one

I had never been fond of the MacElvins' London house. Their much smaller house in Inverness had seemed to me more friendly. But at least the Russell Square house, with its sweeping marble staircase and its ballroom lighted by crystal chandeliers, held no vivid memories for me, painful or otherwise.

Cousin Gertrude and I spent our first days there quietly. Each morning we went for a drive, she with her ear trumpet at hand and smiling vaguely out of the coach window. In the afternoons, while she slept, I again took the air. Usually the coachman, at my direction, drove down the Mall past St. James Palace, and then by a circuitous route through Hyde Park and back to Russell Square.

Even though some of Aunt Dora's friends, notified by her that I was in London, sent invitations to evening parties, I could not accept them, not when Cousin Gertrude retired promptly at eight o'clock each night. But we did take morning coffee at several houses. And when we had been in London a little more than a week, Lady Carter, an old friend of Aunt Dora's, took me to a reception at St.

James Palace. We waited in line in an anteroom until we were admitted to the presence of His Majesty, King George the Second. He was a fat little man with somewhat ribald eyes. When it was my turn to curtsy, he grasped my hand to raise me to my feet. Then, as was his custom when a woman presented to him caught his fancy, he kissed me on the mouth with his plump, rather moist lips. I wondered how many other women had had to restrain the impulse to raise a gloved wrist and wipe the royal kiss from their mouths.

With morning and afternoon drives, and chatter over coffee cups about fashions and scandals, I lived through the days without too much difficulty. It was the evenings that seemed endless. In the sitting room which adjoined my bedroom, I would settle down determinedly to read. But soon, finding that the words made no sense, I would lay the book aside and give myself up to torturing thoughts of John and Charity aboard that ship. Or perhaps, if the wind had favored them, they were already in Boston. Soon the senior Harwoods, overjoyed that their son had turned away from his long attachment to Walter Logan's willful daughter, would welcome the bridal pair to that farmhouse on the hill.

It was midway of my third week in London that I looked out of my coach one day and saw an old friend.

Afternoon traffic was more congested than usual along the Mall that day. As my coach, one of a long line, rolled at a snail's pace down the broad avenue, I became aware of three fashionably dressed men sauntering along the sidewalk. Behind them trailed a small, motley crowd, its members ranging from Londoners as well-dressed as the men they followed to several ragged urchins who looked like chimney sweeps. The tallest of the three men, resplendent in blond peruke and brown velvet coat and breeches, was plainly the object of the crowd's curiosity. With startled disbelief, I realized that he was Charles Edward.

He turned his head, saw me, and said something to his friends. Then he was out in the roadway, opening the door of my coach. "May I?"

I was so glad to see him that it astonished me. "Oh, yes!"

When he was on the seat opposite me, he leaned out the window, waved to the curious crowd, and called to his two companions, "Go on to Lady Primrose's house. I will join you there." He leaned back in the corner and said, as the coach crawled forward "The last time I saw you, you looked like a small rat dragged out of the swamp."

"And you looked like Robinson Crusoe."

He laughed. I saw now that although he was still handsome, he was less lean than I remembered. There were lines at the corners of his brown eyes, and a hint of dissipated fullness beneath them. But the eyes themselves still held that cheerful friendliness.

His appreciative gaze was taking in my green velvet gown, my green hat with its ostrich plume, and the coach's rosewood interior with its mother-of-pearl inlays. "I told you that your face would be your fortune. Your husband must be very rich indeed."

I said, hoping that no pain showed in my face, "I have no husband."

He arched his eyebrows eloquently.

I felt color in my cheeks. "And no—benefactor, at least not of the sort you have in mind. You see, it was discovered that I do have Macduveen blood. My father was illegitimate, unfortunately, but still his father was a Macduveen."

"It was discovered? How?"

"A man who was once in love with my natural great-aunt, Arabella Macduveen, saw how much I resembled her. He and his wife are now my guardians, although I spend more time at Castle Bowain than with them."

"You see? I was right. Your face was your fortune. Tell me, do you still have that coat button I gave you?"

"Of course. It is in my jewel box."

He leaned forward. "Please take supper with me. There is a splendid little inn on the road to Richmond—"

"You know that is impossible."

"Wouldn't you enjoy an hour's conversation with an old friend? Aren't you at least a little curious as to why you find me here, sauntering about the Hanoverian's capital?"

"Of course. But I cannot have supper with you at an inn, and not only for reasons of propriety. The Macduveens are all Whigs and Protestants. So are my guardians, the MacElvins. What would they say if they heard I had been seen having supper with Charles Stuart? I only hope no one who knows me saw you get into this coach. Probably no one did. My acquaintanceship in London is not wide."

He took my hand between both of his, and I, enjoying the warmth of his touch, allowed it to remain there. "Please, Elizabeth! I must return to the Continent tomorrow. Cannot we drink a toast together to auld lang syne and to Bowain Wood?"

I still felt drawn to him, this handsome young man who wore his fine clothes as debonairly, but not more so, as he had worn a frayed coat and kilt. And that day in Bowain Wood he had provided more than a warm fire, and brandy, and a button from his coat. At a time when I was of about as much consequence to others as the courtyard cat, and when he himself was hard-pressed indeed, he had concerned himself with what was to become of me.

And so I sat silent, considering his request. Once Cousin Gertrude had laid her ear trumpet aside and gone to bed, not even a cannon shot would arouse her, let alone the arrival of a guest. Nor would the servants need to know who had visited me. After they, at my request, had set out a light supper—not in the huge dining room, but in my sitting room, where I could serve it myself—I would dismiss them.

The coach had left the crowded Mall now and was moving at a brisker pace along Whitehall. "Could you come to the MacElvin house in Russell Square? It would be best if you came quite late."

"Ten o'clock?"

"Yes." I gave him the house number.

"Thank you, Elizabeth. I will be there. And now, if you will ask your coachman to drive to Lady Primrose's . . ."

He did not leave the coach directly in front of Lady Primrose's house. As he himself pointed out, she had been a well-known—some would say notorious—enthusiast for the Stuart cause. For my coach even to stop at her house, let alone disgorge Charles Edward Stuart, would give rise to speculation that I was a secret Jacobite. And so he left me about a hundred yards away from the house, with its long line of coaches and sedan chairs waiting before it. My own coach turned around. I rode back to Russell Square feeling a little less leaden-hearted than I had for many days.

By eleven that night, Charles and I had consumed all of the turtle soup I had served from a candle-heated tureen, and much of the cold joint and salad, and all but one of three bottles of wine. It had been a merry meal. Almost exclusively, he had talked of his fugitive days in the Highlands. He chuckled over his masquerade as the Irish giantess, Betty Burke, and spoke with affection of the Seven Men of Glenmoriston, those self-proclaimed outlaws who at one period, until the Redcoats drew too close, had provided him with what seemed almost royal comforts in a spacious mountain cave. He did not speak of the campaign that had led up to the disaster at Culloden, nor of his life since he had sailed away from Scotland. With wonder, I realized that for him the high point of his life had been those perilous days when, often cold and hungry, he had eluded capture.

At last I asked, "How is it you are here in London?"

"Not because of a written invitation from St. James, you may be sure." He leaned back in the small red velvet sofa on which he sat, and looked at me wryly across the littered table. "Nevertheless, the English ambassador at Versailles did drop a hint that if I visited London, I would not be clapped into the Tower. I think George wanted me to see what little chance I have of rallying support here."

When he did not go on, I asked tentatively, "And?"

"I have seen what he wanted me to. Lady Primrose and a few others have overwhelmed me with invitations and with expression of undying loyalty. But it is only talk." He looked suddenly tired and older than he had a few minutes before. For the first time I noticed that his red hair, not covered tonight by the blond peruke, had a few threads of gray.

"But you still have hopes that your father—"

"Will sit on the British throne? Almost no hope at all. But I must still make the gestures, must still travel about Europe begging for men and arms. I am James Stuart's son. What else is left for me to be, or do?"

I thought of the lines my father had so often quoted:

> There is a tide in the affairs of men,
> Which taken at the flood, leads on to fortune.

But it was the next two lines which described what had happened to the man who sat opposite me:

> Omitted, all the voyage of their life
> Is bound in shallows and in miseries.

His tide had reached its flood at Derby, with the way to London open before his victorious Highlanders. But he had been persuaded to turn back. And now he was stranded in the shallows, perhaps forever.

He straightened his shoulders, as if throwing off burdensome thoughts. "And now I have a question for you." Once more his eyes were warm and teasing. "How is it that the beauteous Elizabeth Logan, ward of a rich man, wears no wedding band?"

I tried to smile. "Because I have not married."

"Don't fence with an old friend. Has no man won your heart?"

Pain was tightening my throat. "Yes, one has."

"Well?"

"He married someone else."

He looked at me wonderingly. "I should like to see her.

She must be ravishing indeed."

"No." It was hard to breathe now. "She is plain, and very quiet."

"Then why—"

"Because she had what I do not have! Good sense!"

The tears came in a flood. I crossed my arms on the table and pillowed my head upon them.

I felt his hands lifting me from my chair. He led me, sobbing, to the sofa, and drew me down into his arms. "Poor Elizabeth. Poor fledgling. Tell me about it."

Crying in his arms, I told him. My refusal to marry John because he had voted for my father's banishment. The years when I had gone on loving him despite little or no hope of ever seeing him again. My second chance, in Inverness, to marry him, and my failure to grasp it in time.

Stroking my hair, Charles said in a flat voice, "Once the stone is cast, there is no end to the ripples, is there? Because I landed in Scotland, an American I never heard of was banished from a village I never heard of, and his daughter . . ."

He broke off. With his handkerchief he dried my face. He kissed me on the forehead and then, more lingeringly, on the mouth. He said, "More than once these past years I have wondered if I would ever see you again. I hoped that if I did I would find you safe and happy. But perhaps there are no happy endings." He looked down into my eyes. "Only happy intervals, now and then."

Again he kissed me. I was aware of warmth. Warmth of his mouth on my mouth, of his hands through the thin silk of my dress, and of warmth spreading within me. My arms fastened around his neck. I had a sense of being swept along by many forces. The headiness of the wine. A stir of that old grief for my father, so fervent in the cause of the man holding me in his arms. Lonely despair over the happiness I had thrown away. And the growing passion aroused by Charles's hands and lips.

He raised his head and looked down at me. His eyes had changed. Instinctively I was aware that now they were the eyes of a practiced seducer, judging whether or not the moment was right. But that did not seem to matter. I did not protest as he lifted me in his arms and carried me through the doorway to my bed.

When at last we lay quiet, he leaned his head on his elbow-propped hand. Light from the sitting room chandelier gleamed on his bare shoulder. "Elizabeth, I am sorry. I did not know."

"That I had had no lover?"

"Yes. Many women of my acquaintance these past few years— Well, that is no matter. But I realize now that your unhappiness gave me an unfair advantage."

I could not talk of John. Anyone or anything but him. "I should think that you have found little need of added advantages."

His tone was self-mocking. "Oh, yes. Bonnie Prince Charlie. I have read some of those ballads."

Then, soberly: "I cannot marry you, Elizabeth. Whether I like it or not, I am a prince. My father was the son of an anointed sovereign, who in turn was the descendant of a long line of anointed sovereigns. When I marry, it must be with some woman of similar lineage, so that my son may have hope of gaining the British throne, even though that hope has grown thin indeed for my father and for me."

"I realize that."

For a while he was silent, winding a tendril of my hair around one finger. Then he said, "But come with me to the Continent tomorrow. Or join me there as soon as possible. Except that we cannot marry, I will do everything in my power to make you happy."

In my loneliness and sorrow, it was a temptation, but not a great one. I pictured what my life would be as Charles Edward's mistress, wandering with him, a man already too much given to drink, from one capital to another. To annoy the English, some monarch would treat him with the outward respect due royalty. But in the manners I would encounter, the veneer of respect, if there at all, would be thin indeed.

Besides, it was said that he already had a mistress, a certain Clementia Walkinshaw . . .

"No, Charles. I could not bear to have some lawfully married Countess turn her back on me—or have her husband whisper invitations into my ear."

After several moments he said, "You are right, little one. Both those things would happen. And I, whose duty it is to make friends, not enemies, would be able to do little to stop it."

He bent his head and kissed me, gently at first, and then with growing urgency. No happy endings, I thought, only happy intervals. With my lips responding to his, I clasped my arms around his neck.

Twenty-two

For three weeks more I stayed in the Russell Square
house. Cousin Gertrude and I continued to take morning
coffee in various drawing rooms, although for me the chatter about gowns and balls and courtships and other people's marital transgressions long since had become weari-
some. I went driving twice a day. The leaves on the trees
bordering the Mall had become fewer each day, but the
coaches and sedan chairs moving beneath them even more
numerous. Many Londoners who had spent the summer at
their country houses had returned to town.

In the long evenings I still found it hard to read. Again
and again I realized I had turned several pages without ab-
sorbing a word. Instead I had been thinking of John and
Charity. No doubt they were occupying an upstairs room
at the senior Harwoods' house. But had John begun to
build the house he and I had planned, the one farther
along the hill, with a view of the sloping fields and the
bay?

I did not think of Charles Edward often, and when I did
it was with no strong emotion, neither sharp regret for my

transgression, nor longing to repeat it. Perhaps because I had always been aware of the great gulf between us—yes, even when he was a ragged fugitive—those hours I had spent in his arms seemed unreal to me, like a dream I'd had many nights ago.

One morning I awoke, went to my window, and saw London fog, stained with smoke from thousands of chimneys, shrouding the almost naked trees in the garden. Suddenly I was seized with longing for the springiness of heather under my feet, and crystalline air, and the deep blue of lochs. At breakfast I suggested to Cousin Gertrude that we leave London. Her eager acquiescence made me ashamed of myself. She told me, poor lady, that she had been worrying that the leaky roof of her little house in Inverness might be ruining her possessions. Locked in my own concerns, I had not realized that she wanted to go home.

We set out two days later. Since the MacElvins were still away in the West Indies, I spent one night in Cousin Gertrude's house. Fortunately there had not been enough rain for that leak to cause damage. The next morning I set out for Bowain Castle, traveling through the Great Glen along the road that bordered the wide waters of Loch Ness, mirror-smooth on this still day. When I saw the cloud-wreathed bulk of Ben Nevis standing like a guard at the entrance to what I thought of as "my" Highlands, my heart swelled with something almost like happiness. My thoughts sped ahead to my usual homecoming ritual— exchanging a few polite sentences with Lady Macduveen, and then hurrying out to the stables to see Angus, who still called me "lass," and then to the kitchen to greet

Jenny, who now called me "milady."

I had long since made my peace with her. To my surprise, she had confessed readily that she had known I was a Macduveen the moment she saw me. Nor did she, as I had anticipated, try to excuse her silence on the ground that she had not wanted to burden me with the knowledge of my grandmother's "shame." Instead she said forthrightly, "I could not abide that saint-praying woman, or that saucy brat of hers, Walter Logan. If her granddaughter and his daughter was to join the gentry, it was not going to be any of *my* doing. And if it was a sin to keep silent, it will just have to be on my soul." Outrageous as I found her words, I could not help but respect her for refusing to disguise her motives.

I would not be seeing Mag. Soon after I became Ian MacElvin's ward, Mag had run away with a handsome tinker, one of a band of gypsies who had crossed the English border to wander in the Highlands.

When I reached Bowain Castle, I found that even though Donald was absent, Lady Macduveen was not alone. Clarence MacElvin and his wife were there, and had been for several weeks, ever since their manor house had been severely damaged by a fire. I was not dismayed by their presence, even though from the first I had never taken to my guardian's older brother, and had liked him even less after his first wife's diary had come into my possession. I would still have my room and the whole outdoors to wander through. Too, the evening meals, taken in Lady Macduveen's sitting room rather than in the big dining hall with its cavernous fireplace, had always been uncomfortable when there was just Lady Macduveen and myself breaking long silences with trivial conversation. Perhaps the visitors' presence would make those meals livelier.

That proved to be the case. With the MacElvins at table, the talk usually turned to politics, a subject which seemed of even greater interest to Mrs. MacElvin than to her husband. Like most landed aristocrats—her father, I had learned, was an eighth baron, with extensive lands near Edinburgh—she was a staunch Whig. She distrusted that fast-rising statesman, William Pitt, "a wayward Whig, if he is a Whig at all," and still mourned the great Whig Robert Walpole. One evening her talk ranged back thirty-five years to the Stuart Rising of 1715, and to Walpole's firm support at that time of the first Hanoverian monarch, George the First. Since she was obviously several years younger than her husband, she could not have been more than fourteen or fifteen at that time. But from the knowledgeable way in which she spoke, one might have thought that she herself had been on the battlefield at Preston, administering a sound drubbing to all the Stuart forces, including an ex-potboy from Bowain Castle.

"It was disgraceful," she said, her dark eyes flashing. "At that time there were Protestant Scotsmen, even friends of my father's, who supported the Rebels. Not for love of the Stuarts, you may be sure. It was love of French gold that impelled them, and hope that a victorious Stuart king would reward them with their neighbors' lands."

Clarence MacElvin said, "They say that the young Pretender was in London a few weeks ago, strolling along the Mall with a gawking crowd at his heels."

Lady Macduveen said, "Did you hear about that, Elizabeth, while you were in London?"

My nerves tightened. Had someone, after all, recognized me that day Charles got into my coach? But the three faces turned toward me held nothing but casual interest. "Yes, I heard that he had been in London."

"They also say," Clarence went on, "that he attended a church service at St. Mary's in the Strand."

His wife said sardonically, "No doubt to indicate to the English people that the Stuarts would be tolerant of Protestantism."

Lady Macduveen said, "You and Clarence were married in that church, were you not?"

Mrs. MacElvin nodded. "Six years ago last month."

I felt startled. Perhaps because they were both middle-aged, I had assumed they had been married for many years. Why, I wondered, had he waited for so long after Arabella's death to remarry?

It must have been four or five days after that supper table conversation that Donald Macduveen returned for one of his sojourns beneath the ancestral roof. During the past few years he had grown plumper and plumper, so that now he was undeniably fat. But as his girth had increased, the hostility between us had lessened. We were both still young, beneath a roof that sheltered otherwise only middle-aged and elderly gentry and servants. A wider experience of the world had shown me that his behavior toward me that first night, however detestable, was not untypical of his class where a servant girl was concerned. As for those painful slurs he had cast upon my appearance—well, I had observed by now that affronted male self-esteem, as well as female, could lash out cruelly. And so, if we were not friends, we were at least friendly enough that, when Mrs. MacElvin launched into one of her diatribes against Pitt, his eyes and mine could meet in veiled amusement.

He had been at home more than a week when I encountered him on the moor one morning. I had just spent half an hour or so beside my father's grave. As I emerged from the little grove near the grassy clearing, I heard a dog barking. Then I saw it about a quarter of a mile away, straining at a leash held by a young boy. Donald's portly figure, standing beside a sleek bay horse from the castle stable, was recognizable even at that distance. So was Murdock, his hunched figure astride the pony he kept beside the round tower, long beard streaming in the breeze. As I drew close, I saw that Donald held a hooded hawk perched on his leather-gloved fist.

He turned to me, smiling. "Good morning, Elizabeth." His gaze returned to the hawk. "Isn't she beautiful?"

I looked at the hooded, motionless head, the broad breast streaked with black and white, the folded dark wings, the greenish feet with their hooked talons gripping Donald's gloved fist. "What sort of hawk is it?"

"A peregrine falcon, and a fine one."

"From the round tower?" I looked at Murdock. As I had expected, he glared back at me.

"Of course not." Donald sounded irritated. "Will Mac-Cullen loaned her to me." Will MacCullen was one of Donald's drinking companions. "Will loaned me the dog, too. We used to keep hunting dogs, until Mother decided they were a useless expense." He did not mention the shy-looking, sandy-haired boy, although I was sure that he too was from the MacCullen estate.

Donald went on, with growing anger, "I find that our hawks are no longer fit for flying. Murdock should have

198

flown them regularly."

The old man was glaring at Donald now. I felt sorry for the falcon keeper. Why should he, enfeebled with age, have exerted himself to keep the hawks in condition? As far as I knew, this was the first time since I had come to Bowain Castle that the young laird had gone hawking. Too, perhaps the old man had feared to lose his only companions if he launched them into the air. I knew little of falconry, but I did know that sometimes the freed bird does not return to the fist.

His ill humor apparently vented, Donald turned to me with a smile. "Would you like to see me fly her? There is a wood pigeon over in that clump of gorse."

I looked from the peregrine's curved talons to the straining dog and then back again. "No, thank you. I had best—"

"Don't be squeamish, Elizabeth. It is the hawk's nature. And she is beautiful in the air."

Reluctant and yet fascinated, I watched Donald pull the hood from the dark head with its fierce, curved beak and, with a shout of "Wait on!" fling his arm upward. The hawk rose, straight up with legs dangling for a moment, and then in slow circles, each circle carrying her higher. As I watched, head back, I had the sensation that Arabella had described in her diary—a sense that it was I up there, feeling the thrust of air under slowly beating wings.

The hawk was so high now that she looked no larger than a swallow. A few moments later I understood the phrase "Wait on!" While the unleashed dog dashed to the gorse clump and circled it, barking, the hawk continued to make her silent, waiting circles against the brilliant sky.

With a clatter of wings, the wood pigeon flew upward

from the gorse. Obviously the smaller bird was aware of that hovering assassin, because it began a frantic, evasive flight, gliding downward at an angle with wings almost closed, then rising steeply to glide in another direction.

"Watch the hawk!" Donald directed. Then, as I looked upward: "She has turned on her back now. Here is the stoop!"

She was hurtling toward earth, head downward, growing larger each fraction of a second. I saw, or thought I saw, one of her talons strike at the pigeon. But the quarry, in a steep glide, temporarily escaped death. The falcon plunged on and then, checking her descent, began to mount higher and higher in those slow circles. I cried, "The pigeon! Where is it?"

"In that other clump of gorse over there." He looked up at the circling hawk. "I will serve her as soon as she reaches her point."

"Serve her?"

"Flush the quarry out again. The hawk will not miss this time."

I thought of the exausted bird huddled with laboring heart. "Oh, Donald! It tried so hard. It so wants to live. Can't you allow it to?"

"And spoil the hawk? Don't talk nonsense." He nodded to the sandy-haired boy. The boy, who had called the dog back to him when the pigeon rose, again unfastened the leash. The dog dashed to another and more distant clump of gorse and barked until the pigeon again rose and began its evasive flight. But it was obviously tired now, its steep climbs short, its slanting glides less swift.

The falcon plunged. Unable to look away, I saw the talons seize the pigeon and bear it earthward.

"She is about a quarter of a mile away," Donald said. "Wait here."

He mounted the horse and set off at a brisk trot over the moor. I waited with the boy and with Murdock, who seemed to be trying to pretend that I was not there. When Donald rode back, he was carrying the falcon, hooded after her meal, on his fist. The boy lifted from the ground a contraption which Donald referred to as a "cadge," a wooden framework consisting of two poles joined at one end by a wide, flat piece of wood. A leather strap, long enough that the boy could slip it over one shoulder, ran slantwise between the poles. While the boy stood in the cadge, rather like a horse between two shafts, Donald placed the hooded falcon on the platform and tied its leash through a hole in the board.

As the boy, followed by the dog, moved off toward Bowain Castle, Donald called after him, "Take care you don't jostle her too much in the cart! And tell your master I had fine sport." He turned to me. "Would you like to see the hawks in the tower? Murdock has ruined them, of course, but they still might interest you."

The old man, toothless mouth working, began to wave his arms angrily, whether because of the slur on his custodianship or my proposed visit, I did not know. Donald said, laughing, "Go to the devil, you old idiot."

Murdock jerked his pony around, dug his heels into its sides, and galloped toward the tower. Again Donald laughed. "Come on. You can ride pillion."

I hesitated. "He seems very angry."

"What matter if he is? It is not his tower, or his falcons."

"Couldn't we walk there? It is only about half a mile."

"Why walk?" As he lifted me onto the pillion, I reflected that it was little wonder that he was fatter each time I saw him. Even when he did venture out for a day of sport, he exerted himself as little as possible.

As the horse moved slowly across the moor, Donald said in a voice that blended sympathy with curiosity, "Mother tells me that you went to London because you had had a disappointment. Something about a man you used to know in America. I was sorry to hear it."

So Aunt Dora must have written to Bowain Castle to explain my stay in London. Lady Macduveen had never mentioned the letter to me. I knew that her silence had arisen, not from delicacy, but a refusal to become involved in anyone else's pain. I said, "Yes, but I would rather not talk about it."

"All right. I will talk about something more cheerful. Someone told Will MacCullen that Charles Stuart was seen getting into your coach on the Mall."

He must have heard my swift intake of breath, because he added, "Don't worry. I have not told Mother. And I certainly will not tell Clarence MacElvin and that Jacobite-eating wife of his." He paused. "Or don't you want to talk about Stuart, either?"

I did not, and not just because I feared talk of the London episode might reach the ears of the Clarence MacElvins and of my guardian and Aunt Dora. That interval in my bedroom in the Russell Square house no longer seemed like a fading dream. Of late I'd had reason to think of it often, and uneasily.

I said, "There is nothing to tell. He left the coach near Lady Primrose's house, and then I went home." I continued swiftly, "You mentioned the MacElvins. The other night I learned that they had been married for only six years. I wonder why Clarence MacElvin remained unmarried for so long after his first wife's death."

Donald laughed. "Probably he was waiting to find a woman with sufficiently good prospects. Her father is almost eighty, and a very rich man."

Donald's surmise struck me as probably correct. Clarence MacElvin's first marriage to a beautiful and unwilling young woman had ended in tragedy. It was little wonder that he had chosen as his second wife an heiress in her forties.

We had reached the round tower. Donald dismounted, helped me to the ground, and tethered the horse to the corner post of the pony's pen. The pony wore a collar, I saw now, which consisted of a cloth-padded chain. Attached to the collar was another chain which ran to an iron ring set in the tower's rounded wall. Following the direction of my gaze, Donald said, "Murdock has always been afraid someone will steal that bag of bones. He keeps it chained up like that and hides the key somewhere in the tower."

Moving to the wide wooden door, he pulled the latchstring. The door did not swing open. "Damn the old fool!" He hammered with his fist. "Murdock! Unbar the door!"

After a moment I heard the grate of wood against wood. The door swung open. Murdock stood there in an arc of sunlight. He looked, not angry now, but merely sullen. Turning his back on us, he walked to a stool set against the curving stone wall, sat down, and crossed his arms over his chest. Donald left the door open, for which I was glad. Against the wall, near the entrance to the stairs, stood a wooden rake and shovel, intended for use, I suppose, in keeping the dirt floor clean. But Murdock must have employed them seldom, because the room smelled strongly of bird droppings, as well as of Murdock.

Even I could tell that the hawks, moving restlessly on their long perch and blinking in the unaccustomed sunlight, were not healthy. They were lusterless both of eye and plumage. Donald identified them for me. There was a small hobby and an even smaller merlin, "good only for flying at larks." There was a huge gyrfalcon, its white plumage dotted with black, and a peregrine falcon so dull of feather that I scarcely would have recognized it as the same sort of bird that had hurtled from the sky to seize the pigeon in its talons.

At last I said, "Could I see the rest of the tower?" As I spoke, I glanced at Murdock, half expecting him to leap to his feet and protest with waving arms this further violation of what he plainly considered his property. Instead, he merely glowered at me.

Donald shrugged. "There is not much to see—only three rooms, one on each floor."

We went up curving stairs, their stone steps hollowed out by the feet of armed defenders and perhaps invaders, centuries dead. The room directly above the falcons' lair was unmistakably Murdock's. I stood in the doorway, breathing shallowly in the fetid air. Sunlight, slanting through the arrow slits, showed me his bed—a pallet and a tangle of blanket—on the floor strewn with straw. Beneath one of the arrow slits stood a small iron brazier. Probably he used it, not only for cooking, but to combat the bone-chilling cold of winter.

Gladly I turned away and followed Donald up to the

next room. Its door was closed, but opened easily under his hand. I peered in at iron-bound wooden chests, their lids piled with wooden boxes and what looked like rolled-up carpets or tapestries. The room above contained similar chests and storage boxes. I asked, "Did you ever look into all of those containers?"

"Yes, when I was fifteen. Mostly they hold dresses and coats and breeches so fallen to pieces that my grandmother must have had them placed here. But I did find two old swords and a pistol. Those I took away with me." He laughed. "When Murdock came up to see what I had been doing, he was so angry that I thought he was going to fly at me with his fists."

We climbed the last flight of stairs and opened a heavy wooden door onto the slate-covered roof. As the door swung to behind us, I noticed that there was a heavy iron bar affixed to the wood, rusting in its brackets. I said, "I wonder why they wanted to bar this door from the outside?"

"I suppose in the event the tower's defenders were driven up to the roof. With the door barred, they would have a few additional moments to prepare for a final stand."

It was hard to realize that this tower, empty now except for an old man, drooping falcons, and chests and boxes of moldering garments, had once echoed to the clash of swords and the shouts of men fighting on stone stairs slippery with blood.

Donald had moved over to the deeply crenelated parapet. I joined him and looked down the sheer drop of sixty feet. "Until I was about eighteen," he said, "I used to climb from here to the ground whenever the notion struck me."

It seemed incredible that the man beside me had ever been slender and agile enough to perform such a feat. "Wasn't that very dangerous?"

"Not as dangerous as you might think. You can see there are crevices between the stones. They were my fingerholds and toeholds. And in some places the outward course of stones had fallen away entirely. Too, you can see how the base of the tower begins to slope outward about twenty feet from the ground. Once I was down that far, the rest of the descent was not difficult.

"Besides," he went on, "sometimes I held onto a rope while I went from one foothold to another." He looked to his right and then laughed. "Why, part of it is still there!"

I looked at the once-stout rope, one of its ends tied through a ring bolt affixed to the top of a crenelation. From there it dangled, sun-bleached to a pale yellow and frayed in many places, to a point a few feet above where the tower began to widen. I imagined the young and slender Donald descending along that rope, feet searching for crevices and hollows in the rocky wall. . . .

Dizziness assailed me. I clung to the parapet with both hands.

He said in an alarmed voice, "Are you going to faint? You're as white as a fish's belly."

I turned and leaned my back against the parapet. Nausea was stirring in me now. "Perhaps I will be all right in a moment."

"You should not have looked down. Evidently you have a poor head for heights."

I had an excellent head for heights. Only last summer I had climbed up a narrow glen, made my way along a ridge to a bluff overlooking the loch where Arabella had drowned herself, and sat there on a wide, sun-warmed rock which projected from the face of the bluff.

"We had best go down," Donald said.

"Yes, that would be best."

Twenty-three

On a lowering afternoon nearly two weeks later, I stood at the window of my room, forcing myself to think calmly of my future.

For more than a week now, I had awakened each morning to the grim certainty that I was with child. At first the knowledge had sent my thoughts scattering in panic. After that there had been days of useless regret, when I walked over the moors wondering if any other woman had committed two such follies in the space of a few weeks. Of the two follies—setting my will against that of the man I loved, and then succumbing utterly to a man I merely liked—it seemed to me that the first folly was the greater, because it had prepared me for the second. Charles Edward had been right. My lonely unhappiness, rendering me reckless, had been his ally that night.

But now, since I had no intention of following Arabella into that loch, I had set myself to considering the other alternatives before me. I could seek out Charles Edward on the Continent. But I sensed that his emotions, although strong, were evanescent, at least where women were concerned. Because he was generous, he would befriend me. But he would not welcome the arrival of a pregnant young woman who, more than likely, had been crowded from his thoughts now by his mistress and perhaps by other women. Besides, since I had rejected the idea of myself as part of his idle, wandering life, how could I accept it for my child?

On the other hand, I could not remain at Bowain Castle. Unwilling to concern herself with even the minor troubles of others, Lady Macduveen would never tolerate my embarrassing presence during the time ahead. Nor would it be fair to inflict myself upon my guardians, even if they allowed me to, which they well might not. I felt that, fond as they were of me, there was a distinct possibility that now they would disown me.

But of one thing I felt sure. Neither Ian MacElvin nor Aunt Dora would want to strip me of that five thousand pounds. Properly invested, it would support my child and me in modest comfort. But support us where? Obviously in some place where I might represent myself as a widow. Scotland was not such a place, or even London, since I was known to friends of my guardians there. I would have to cross the Channel to some city in France or the Low Countries. Perhaps in time I would meet some quiet, decent man who would want to become a husband to me and a father to my child.

The calm my decision brought me was a bleak one. It would be hard indeed to leave foaming burns, and mountains changing in the ever-changing light, and heather underfoot, for lodgings on a gray street in some foreign city.

How still everything was. Except for the crackle of a small fire on the hearth, the room seemed as silent as the snow which had begun to fall in large, widely spaced flakes past the window. Down in the kitchen, pots must be banging, and perhaps Jennie was berating Morag, a timid woman with a harelip who had replaced the errant Mag. But no sounds from below or from the courtyard penetrated this room. Nor did I, as I often did at this hour, hear the notes of the spinet in Lady Macduveen's apartment, or Donald's heavy tread in the hall, or Belzebub's deep, bell-like bark. Lady Macduveen, one of the servants had told me, was confined to her bed by a headache. As for Donald, he had gone with the Clarence Mac-Elvins to inspect the repairs on their fire-damaged house. I had seen the coach depart that morning for the eight-mile journey, with the giant hound trotting beside the horses.

Such silence was oppressive. Best to go out, even though snow was falling and the short November day nearing its end. Always I had found that out of doors my heart was a little less heavy. I put on a fur-hooded cloak, walked down the corridor past the dining hall where a fire burned in the huge fireplace, past the closed door to Lady Macduveen's rooms, and down the circular stairs to the entrance tunnel that ran through the castle's thick foundation.

When I emerged from it, I found that what wind there was blew from the east, slanting snowflakes into my face. I walked with lowered head down the narrow road leading to the highroad. With my gaze fixed on the thin layer of snow underfoot, I was unaware of an approaching coach until I heard the sound of its wheels. I moved to the road's edge, expecting to see the MacElvins and Donald drive past. A moment later I saw that the coach was smaller than the MacElvins', and drawn by one roan horse and one bay, rather than the MacElvins' matched grays. Then I saw the face looking out at me from the window. After seeming to stop for a moment, my heart set up a wild, incredulous pounding.

The coach traveled a few more yards before it stopped. The door opened, and he strode toward me, his face so alight with joy that I went, heedless, straight into his arms. He kissed me, and then stood pressing my head against his shoulder. Several moments passed before I even thought to ask, "Then you and Charity are not—"

"No. *She* broke our troth, Elizabeth! I did not tell her of your letter, but she must have sensed that something had happened to make me regret having asked her to marry me. The day after the ship sailed from Glasgow, she told me that she felt we could never find contentment together, let alone happiness."

Remembering the yearning look her gentle eyes had sent him across the MacElvins' Inverness drawing room, I knew how much that decision must have cost her.

"We were becalmed nearly a week, so it was already October by the time we reached Boston. I had to wait nearly two weeks for passage back to Glasgow. Then in Inverness I found the MacElvins' house closed, and so I hired a coach in the hope I would find you here."

October. He had reached Boston in October. I had not left London until mid-October.

Awareness of my situation returned to me, replacing that unthinking joy I had felt at first sight of him. I began to shiver. It must have been too dark for him to see my expression, because all he said was, "You are cold. We must get out of this snow."

In the coach he put his arm around me. I rested my head against his shoulder, unable to deny myself these last few moments of closeness to him. I even tried to pretend that I was the same as when we had parted, and that soon we would marry, and then I would go, not to some lonely lodging on a foreign street, but home to America with my husband.

When the coach rattled over the stones paving the entrance tunnel, I stopped pretending. I lifted my head from his shoulder and straightened my disarranged hood. He asked, "Is there someplace where the coachman could spend the night?"

I said in a taut voice, "Best to have him wait here for a while."

John seemed to realize then that there was something wrong. Face worried, he handed me down from the coach and followed me up the stairs. In the corridor I said, "There is a fire in the dining hall. It will be warm there."

Fresh logs had been added to the fire. Evidently Lady Macduveen, because of her headache, intended to have her son and the Clarence MacElvins take supper here after their return. I indicated one of the two high-backed chairs flanking the fireplace. "Please wait here. I will be back in a moment."

In my room I started to arrange two chairs before the fire as a drying rack for my damp cloak. Then, aware that I had been trying to delay the inevitable moment, I hung my cloak in the wardrobe and went back to the hall. As I entered, John rose from his chair beside the fire. He said in a voice harsh with anxiety, "Something is very wrong. Tell me!"

"Sit down, John." I sat down in the chair opposite him,

and after a moment forced myself to begin to speak. After a few sentences I saw such incredulous pain in his face that I lowered my eyes. I did not look at him again until I had finished my account. I saw that his face was white, and his lips compressed into a thin line.

He said, "And it was to hear this that I re-crossed an ocean!"

As I looked at him wordlessly, he demanded, "Was it not enough to be the daughter of a bastard? Do you have to give birth to one?"

He rose then and walked out. I huddled there, helpless to rise from the chair or make any movement at all. After a few moments I heard the hired coach rattle into the courtyard, turn, and go out through the tunnel.

Twenty-four

I do not know how long I sat there, hearing no sound but the hiss of logs in the grate. For the rest of my life I would see his face at that last moment, and hear his words. I loved him. If these past five years had taught me anything, it was that I would always love John Harwood. How could I live with the memory of loathing in his eyes?

It must have been such grinding misery as this which sent Arabella into the loch.

The thought frightened me. I did not want to take my life and the life of my child. Even in the extremity of my suffering, I knew that it would moderate itself in time.

But as I sat there, the pain did seem more than I could bear. I could not remain here. The torment would be no less, though, in my room—Arabella's room. Arabella, who had lost whatever battle she herself had waged against despair.

My father. All I had now was the memory of my father's love and the hope of my unborn child's. I would go to his grave. Up there I might find some assuagement. And I would see Arabella's grave, reminding me of what could happen to those of insufficient strength. I went down the corridor and tapped softly on the door leading to Lady Macduveen's rooms. When one of the elderly maids opened the door, her face holding determination that her mistress not be disturbed, I said, "Will you please tell Lady Macduveen and the others that I will not be at table? I feel unwell."

She nodded and closed the door.

In my room, I took down a dry cloak from the wardrobe. Swiftly, lest I encounter the old footman moving toward the dining hall to set the long table, I walked down the corridor and descended the south tower stairs. When I reached the courtyard, I found that the temperature had dropped sharply. The kitchen door was closed on this cold night. So were the doors of the outbuildings beyond the courtyard, although from inside the carriage house came the clang of old Angus's hammer, perhaps against a wheel rim. I went on past the last of the outbuildings and then started across the undulating moor.

The snowfall, sparse to begin with, had almost ceased. I would not dare to stay long beside my father's grave. If the cloud cover lifted, icy cold from the polar regions might settle down, that deadly cold which sometimes grips northern Scotland in the winter months. Already my cheekbones ached. I trudged on over the light, crisp snow cover, John's face as it had looked at that last moment always before my eyes. Better, far better, that he had married Charity. Then he and I would have been spared the ugliness of our last meeting.

Aware that the dull gleam of the snow had brightened, I looked up. The polestar, so much higher in Scotland's heavens than in Southampton's, glittered against a black sky. I could also see, in a black lake bordered by tattered clouds, the gleam of Aldebaran, the red eye of the Bull. Lowering my gaze, I trudged on. I forced myself to think of the immediate future. It would be best to tell my guardian and Aunt Dora as soon as possible after they returned to Scotland. Once across the Channel, I would require time to find somewhere to live and to prepare for the birth of my child.

A numb feeling, not unpleasant, had replaced the ache in my cheekbones. Even though I did not look up, I knew that more clouds had cleared from the star-brilliant sky. The white, undulating moor glittered now, like some vast frozen sea.

Must I change my name? And if so, to what? It was odd. So many names I might choose from, and the only one I could think of was Elizabeth Logan.

Not only my face, but my mittened hands and my feet felt that pleasant numbness. And I was so drowsy. If I could just lie down for a few minutes, curled up in my cloak . . .

Deep in my mind, a frantic alarm sounded. I looked at the grove of trees, black against the snow, which stood between me and my father's grave. The grove with its inadequate shelter was at least half a mile ahead. I turned and looked at Bowain Castle, its dark bulk rising nearly three miles away above the seaward edge of the snow-whitened moor. Long before I retraced my steps, I would have succumbed to this drowsy prelude to death.

I looked to my left. Only a few hundred yards away, light shone through arrow slits in the round tower. Murdock up there in his frowzy room, cooking his solitary meal.

I moved toward the tower as fast as I could, numb feet stumbling now and then. Once I blundered into a clump of frozen, snow-covered gorse, and had to free my cloak from its spiny grasp. As I approached the tower door, the shaggy pony, blanketed against the cold, poked his head over the top rail of his pen.

I tried the latch, awkwardly grasping the string with my numb, mittened fingers. I heard the latch lift, but the door did not yield to the push of my other hand. The door was barred. I hammered with both fists against the wood. "Murdock! It is Elizabeth Logan. Let me in!"

No sound for a moment. And then a harsh, inhuman cry. The gyrfalcon? Perhaps. But the cry, although surely not uttered by a human throat, did not sound like that of any sort of bird.

The cry was not repeated. Nor was there any sound of movement beyond the door. "Murdock! If you leave me to freeze out here, you will pay for it!"

Still no response. The crazy old man was going to let me die, only inches from shelter. I continued to pound, not so much from hope as to fight off that growing numbness.

A grating sound as the bar slid back. The door opened. The upward-striking light of the lantern Murdock held made the eyes in his sullen face look like dark holes. I pushed past him into the fetid but blessedly warmer room. The birds moved restlessly on their perches. I said, "I am going to stay here until morning."

He shrugged, closed and barred the door, and pointed to the wooden stool against the wall. As I moved toward it, he walked to the foot of the stairs, set the lantern down on the floor, and started to climb the steps.

It was then that I saw it, the shape of a narrow hand printed in some damp, sticky substance on the back of his ragged sheepskin coat. A child's hand? No, the fingers were too long.

Someone was up there. Somewhere in the tower, this crazy, hate-filled old man kept a human prisoner. "Murdock!"

Already on the third step of the stairs, he turned. Almost instantly I realized the folly of that impulsive cry. The mingled rage and fear in his face told me that he had read my own face, and knew that something had betrayed him.

Paralyzed, I watched him come rapidly down the steps and seize the handle of the wooden shovel. But when he raised it above his head with both hands, the paralysis left me. As he rushed at me, I stooped, grasped the stool by one leg, and flung it straight at his head. He toppled backward, the shovel flying from his hands. I heard the hollow, sickening sound the back of his head made against the bottom step.

One hand propped against the wall's cold stones, I stood there for a moment, fighting off faintness. Had I killed him? At last I was able to cross to where he lay and kneel beside him. Blood was oozing now from a cut on his forehead. I removed one mitten and forced myself to thrust my hand beneath the sheepskin coat and his woolen shirt. His heart still beat, weakly but regularly.

Without opening his eyes, he moved his head. My nerves tightened with fear, not for him now, but for myself. He might regain consciousness before I found the person who had uttered that inhuman cry and then, as a mute plea for help, had left that imprint on the back of his coat.

I looked around. Hanging from an iron spike driven into the wall near the stair entrance was a coil of rope. I took it down and bound him as securely as I could, first the bony old wrists, and then the ankles in their dirt-encrusted woolen stockings. I picked up the lantern and mounted the stairs.

Holding the lantern high, I stood in the doorway of Murdock's room. Nothing but the floor's moldy straw, and the pallet with its tangled blankets, and the brazier in which a fire smoldered, giving off the acrid smell of peat. I went up to the next flight. Here the door had been closed from the outside with a wooden bar. The bar slid back under my hand, and the door swung inward.

Lantern light glittered on the eyes of the woman huddled on the floor, and shone dully on her long, tangled gray hair and the iron gag distorting her mouth.

Unable to move, I thought, "Why, she is so very old!" Somehow, as I climbed the stairs, I had been thinking of Murdock's stepdaughter, the "poor, motherless girl with hair as lusterless as dried straw" whom Arabella had described in her diary. Had she, in spite of that grave in the Garlaig churchyard, remained alive these past thirty-five years, the prisoner of her crazy stepfather? But no. Not even thirty-five years ago could that pitiable creature on the floor have been termed a "girl," especially by Arabella, who at twenty-one had been scarcely more than a girl herself. This woman looked to be at least Murdock's age.

I went into the room, set the lantern down, and knelt beside her on the straw. I took off my other mitten and with shaking, clumsy fingers felt under the matted hair and found the screw that held the gag in place. I unscrewed it and, as carefully as I could, removed the cruel contraption. The part that went over the tongue, I saw now, consisted of a leather strap. With a shudder, I dropped the gag onto the straw. As I did so, I noticed the iron cuff encircling the slender left ankle beneath the tattered hem of her woolen dress. From the cuff a chain ran to a ringbolt in the wall. Her hands, too, were loosely manacled, their iron cuffs joined by a chain about two feet long.

She opened her mouth, trying to speak, and I saw the calloused, swollen tongue. Wonder in her eyes, she pointed to my face and then to her own.

I sat motionless with shock, my gaze going over the features which, I realized now, had been aged far, far beyond their actual years. The eyes, red-rimmed and swollen, but still blue, still wide-spaced. The straight nose. The chin with the scarlike cleft which once must have been a dimple. The small mole at one corner of the pale, withered mouth.

I said, my heart filled with horror and pity, "Arabella?"

"Who—ah—ah—"

Her tongue could not manage the "r" sound, but I understood. "I am your grand-niece, Elizabeth Logan."

She did not seem to hear, much less understand that. She continued to gaze at me with wonder. To her, deprived of a mirror for perhaps decades, it must seem that her ghostly twin had materialized beside her.

Deprived. I looked around this room, in which she had lived deprived of almost everything that pertained to humanity. Chests still stood against the rounded walls, with rolled-up carpets and boxes still piled atop them. In which of those chests, I wondered, had Murdock hidden his prisoner the day that Donald, over the old man's violent protests, had brought me to the tower? He also had hidden her pallet and blankets, now spread out a few feet away, and the wooden bowl, still half filled with gruel, close beside her on the floor.

He must have been feeding her tonight with that wooden spoon lying there on the straw when I hammered on the tower door. She had let out that one hoarse cry before he had slipped the gag back into place. She must have struggled, distracting his attention enough so that she was able to dip her palm into the gruel and leave its imprint on his back.

My sickened gaze continued to roam the room. I saw something else that I had not seen the day I came here with Donald—that tattered leather screen near one of the chests. Behind it, I knew, must be the bucket or other utensil provided for her necessities. The chain fastened to her ankle, although not long enough for her to reach an arrow slit and show her face there, was sufficiently long for her to reach the screen, that one concession to her humanity.

The full horror smote me then. Arabella, who had roamed the moors with the same joy that I had. Arabella, with her quick mind, and her love of poetry, and her passionate, unruly heart. For more than four years, ever since I had first read her diary, I had mourned the thought of all that beauty and sensitive intelligence going to its death in the loch. Now I wished that it had.

I turned back to the woman I knew was in her middle fifties, even though she appeared to be eighty. I inspected the irons on her wrists and her ankle. There were no locks. They would have to be struck from her. I said, "You are going to be free. But I must wait until morning to get you away from here. Murdock's pony is tethered by a locked chain. And it is very, very cold tonight. If I try to walk to the castle for help, I will freeze to death. Do you understand?"

She nodded. The joy in her eyes made them look younger. "Murdock? Dead?" Even though her tongue distorted the words, I understood them.

"No. But he is injured, and he is bound hand and foot. He cannot harm us." I paused. "Who did this to you? Your husband?"

The Arabella of the diary was still alive somewhere within her. Hate leaped into her eyes. She nodded.

"How long have you been here? How many years?"

She hesitated, and then held up six fingers. Six years. I imagined her measuring them by the changing angles of the sun's first rays through the arrow slits, and by the alternation of winter cold with the comparative warmth of full summer.

"Where were you before that?" When I found her reply unintelligible, I asked, "Somewhere on Clarence MacElvin's lands?"

She nodded.

Perhaps he had kept her, gagged and chained, in some remote part of the manor house, her presence known only to himself or to some servant bound to him through money, or shared guilt, or both. Perhaps he had kept her in some separate building. Wherever her prison had been, I thought grimly, soon all Scotland would know about it.

But one thing was clear. Six years ago he had brought

her here. Why? What had happened six years ago? Of course. Six years ago Clarence had taken unto himself, bigamously, a wife who possessed not only rich prospects but a cool intelligence. Arabella's presence, no matter how well hidden, had become too dangerous to him. And so, perhaps under cover of a long winter night, he had installed her here with the mute old falcon keeper as her jailer.

I said, "Why? Why did Clarence MacElvin do this to you?"

Again that flash of hatred. "Treason," she said, almost distinctly.

"He was a traitor?" She nodded. "To the Hanoverians?" Again she nodded. "Took—French gold."

French gold. It was in large part French gold which had financed that Stuart Rising thirty-five years ago, in 1715. Clarence MacElvin, that seeming staunch supporter of the Protestant succession, had taken King Louis's money. And in return for it? In return he must have given a secret pledge to support with his arms and those of his tenants the exiled Catholic Stuarts.

But when the Rising actually came, he had not kept his promise, probably because of a belated realization that the rebellion was bound to fail. He had remained in the eyes of everyone a staunch supporter of the Protestant monarchy until—months after the 1715 Rising had been crushed—an agent of the French had appeared to remind him of that broken promise. And with her ear pressed to the closed drawing room door, the young bride who hated him had learned of the treason that could cost him his head.

Even now, I realized, it could cost him his head. Only

three years before a certain Lord Derwentwater had been beheaded, not for any part in the 1745 Rising led by Charles Edward, but in the 1715 Rising led by Charles's father.

Sitting here now beside the broken creature my great-aunt had become, I realized that all along I should have guessed the nature of what she had discovered. In her much-underlined copy of *King Richard the Third*, in a scene dealing with another indecisive turncoat named Clarence, she had made a double line beneath the words "false, fleeting, perjured Clarence." I could imagine how, after listening to that conversation between her husband and the French agent, she had gone up to her room, made that last entry in her diary, and then with bitter triumph—remembering the swift if informal execution of that other Clarence—opened her copy of the play to slash twice with her pen under that line.

Whether or not Clarence MacElvin had been forced to return the French gold might never be known at this late date. Probably he had, with interest. But there was little doubt what had happened to Arabella. Late in the afternoon the day after she wrote that last entry in her diary, she had gone for a walk on the moors and never returned. Was it her husband alone who had seized her and carried her off to some place of imprisonment, or had he been aided by the comparatively young Murdock of thirty-five years before? Probably the latter, I decided, and probably Murdock had kept her for a few weeks here in the tower, while Clarence MacElvin went off to London to show himself prominently in public places. He had still been in London when, about two weeks after Arabella's disappearance, the body of a yellow-haired young woman had gone into the loch. He had still been there when, about a week later, that body had washed ashore.

I had no doubt whose body it had been—that stepdaughter of Mudock's, the girl with the strawlike hair. Had Murdock deliberately killed her and then placed her body in the deepest part of the loch, where it would take days to wash ashore? I did not think so. For one thing, if Murdock had agreed to kill her, there would have been no need to delay two weeks before placing her body in the loch. No, it must have been plain to both men that the girl was near death, and that it would be better if the body, when eventually found, bore no marks of mortal wounds or of strangulation. And so Murdock had waited until she ceased to breathe. He had dressed her then in the clothes Arabella wore when she left the castle for the last time. Perhaps he had placed Arabella's rings on her fingers.

When the body of a yellow-haired girl in Arabella's clothes, with a face bloated beyond recognition, was washed ashore, the bereaved husband had rushed back from London. Here he had resisted demands that she be given a suicide's burial at the crossroads, and had consented, finally, to the lonely gravesite on the moor.

But why? Why had he not eliminated, coldly and decisively and forever, the wife who could have sent him to the block? I hesitated, and then asked, "Why did he let you live?"

A look of profound irony shone in her eyes, and faintly curved her pale lips. She had to repeat her answer twice before I understood it. "He did not want that sin on his soul."

Perjury, yes. Treason, yes, and bigamy. But not wife-murder. And so he, chronically self-divided, chronically a taker of half measures, had condemned her to an existence from which she often must have longed for the release of death.

Was it only greed which had induced the old falcon keeper to become Arabella's jailer? I thought not. No doubt Clarence had paid him well for placing his step-daughter's wasted body in the loch. No doubt Clarence had paid him again when he brought Arabella here six years ago. But surely it was fear more than money which had made him guard his prisoner so closely—fear that if her presence here were revealed, he might be accused of murdering that girl with the straw-yellow hair.

I became aware that Arabella had turned her ravaged face toward the pallet. I asked, "Do you want to lie down?" She nodded. Plainly the shock of my sudden appearance here, and her efforts to communicate with me, had exhausted her small store of strength. She began to move crabwise across the floor, palms of her chained hands flat on the straw, and dragging her legs after her. Filled with revulsion and pity, I helped her onto the pallet and covered her with the rough blanket.

It was so cold in here. Evidently she was inured to it, but I, even in my heavy cloak, was conscious of the icy air. Perhaps that wooden-handled brazier in the room below was not too heavy to lift. If so, I would bring it up here. I carried the lantern down to the next landing, left it there, and entered Murdock's room.

The brazier was not too heavy. I carried it out to the stone landing. There I paused, struck by a chill thought. What if, after I left him, the old man's heart had ceased to beat? I set down the brazier with its dully glowing contents, and went down the stairs.

226

On the bottom step I stopped and stood motionless. Enough lantern light shone down from the landing above to show me that the rope now lay loosely coiled on the dirt floor, and that the door stood open to the freezing night.

How much time had passed since he freed himself from those inexpertly knotted bonds? Enough time for him to ride to the castle? Heart hammering, I ran outside. The pony was gone from his pen.

Hearing the sound of hoofbeats, I whirled around.

Black against the snow, a horse and its rider were racing toward me. No need to wonder who the rider was. And now at long last he could not afford half measures. If he wanted to escape the headsman's ax, he would have to silence forever both that helpless chained creature and me.

Twenty-five

I darted back into the room where the falcons rustled, slammed the heavy door, and groped for its wooden bar. The bar was gone.

Feeling cold perspiration roll down my sides, I leaned my back against the door. How much time did I have until he burst in upon us? Two minutes? Three? And with what weapon could I defend us? I looked through the dim light at the wooden shovel lying on the floor. Of what use would that be against the pistol he undoubtedly carried?

I ran up the stairs. On the first landing I seized the lantern's bail and then, with my already encumbered left hand and my right, carried the brazier up to the next landing. As I set the lantern down, I glanced through the open door at the thin figure beneath the blanket. No time to hide her, as Murdock had, in one of those chests piled high with boxes and rolled carpets. No time to warn her, and anyway what purpose would a warning serve? Chained hand and foot, she could not defend herself. I could only hope that her husband, intent upon dealing with the less helpless of us, would not stop first to fasten his hands around her thin neck or bludgeon her with a pistol butt.

Now even up here I could hear the muffled beat of hooves. They grew loud, then came to an abrupt halt. As rapidly as I could with the brazier in my hands, I climbed a few more steps and then halted, hidden from below by the curving wall. As he started up this flight, he would be silhouetted against the light of the lantern on the landing below. If I could catch him by surprise . . .

Booted feet on the stairs. I waited, gripping the brazier handles. I could hear my own heartbeats now, more rapid than those climbing footsteps, and almost as loud. I heard him pass Murdock's room without stopping, climb the second flight, and then pause. I knew he must be peering in at that thin shape on the pallet. In agonized apprehension, I waited to hear his footsteps cross the landing, waited to hear her last, helpless cry.

Instead I heard him climbing upward. Two steps. Three. Four.

I came around the curve. He must have fired the instant he saw me. I heard the clang of the pistol ball against the brazier's side, and felt the shock of its impact travel through my hands up to my shoulders. Tipping the brazier, I flung its smoldering contents straight at him.

With a cry of rage and alarm, he flung up crossed arms to protect his face, lost his balance, and went over backward. The pistol clattered from his hand. I saw him slide, headfirst, the short distance to the landing.

Carrying the empty brazier by one handle, I moved swiftly toward him. If I were able to strike him over the head before he could retrieve and reload that pistol . . .

I saw him roll to one elbow, saw his other hand dart under his dark greatcoat. Too late, I remembered that pistols were carried in pairs. Instinctively, just as he fired, I flattened myself against the curving wall. The ball went by my face so close that I felt, or imagined I felt, the faint wind of its passing.

He was getting to his feet now. I caught a glimpse of his face, pale and terrible in the lantern light. I flung the empty brazier at him and then, not waiting to see with what effect I had struck him or if I had struck him at all, I raced up the stairs, pushed open the heavy door, and emerged into the cold, starry dark. I slammed the door closed and began to struggle with that rusted bar. If the brazier had hit his head and rendered him even briefly unconscious, I might have time to shove the bar home.

With a grating sound, the bar moved perhaps an inch, then another inch. I threw all my weight behind my straining hands. He must be unconscious, for I heard no pound of booted feet on the stairs. The iron bar slid, so suddenly that I staggered, into the bracket affixed to the stone wall.

I leaned, panting, against the barred door. Still no sound from beyond it. *Was* he unconscious? Or was he reloading the pistols?

Then, in my mind's eye, I had an unbearable vision of him moving toward the chained creature on the pallet. Had I bought my own life—and perhaps only a few additional minutes of it—at the cost of hers?

Rapid footsteps mounting the stairs now. I felt the door give under the pressure of his hands. The pressure ceased. Then he must have run at it with his shoulder, because the whole door shuddered. I heard one of the rusted bolts that held the bar brackets give way and clatter to the slate tiles. Soon he would have the door open.

I moved away from it then, flung back my head, and screamed hopelessly at the star-brilliant sky. I heard him strike the door again. More than one bolt clattered to the tiles.

There was only one hope, a hope so thin it scarcely deserved the name. I ran to the parapet, stepped up onto the space between two of the tall crenelations, and grasped that dangling rope, first with my right hand, then my left. It had frozen to almost the stiffness of wire. Trying not to think of that sixty feet of empty black space between me and the ground, I stepped off the parapet and hung there, facing the tower's stone side. My toes felt for a niche between the stones, and found one. Above me, I could still hear his shoulder battering against the door. I lowered my hands slightly on the rope and groped with my right foot for another toehold. I found it. It seemed wide enough for the toes of both my shoes. Aware that my palms already must have lost skin to that icy rope, I lowered my left foot to the niche.

Above me, the door burst open.

The rope! All he would have to do would be to loosen it from the ring bolt.

I would have to let go of the rope.

Each separate nerve, each ounce of my flesh, seemed to shrink with the knowledge that if my hand or foot slipped, I would plunge to my death on the tower's outward curving base. My right hand released the rope, felt for a crevice, and instead found a hollow, rough with mortar, where a stone had once been.

But I could not let go of the rope with my left hand. I

simply could not.

I felt a tremor along the rope's length. He had seen me. And now he was untying the rope.

With the courage of despair, I transferred my left hand to that rough hollow. Not daring to look up or down, I closed my eyes and clung with cheek pressed to an icy stone.

He must have seen my movement, or at least realized that now the rope dangled free. Would he lean over the parapet and send a pistol ball crashing into my head?

An eternity passed, perhaps as much as fifteen seconds. No sound from above. Suddenly I realized he need not fire at me, need not risk being charged with my murder. He need not do anything but wait—wait until my fingers, already so numb that I no longer could feel the mortar's roughness, lost their hold entirely, and I plunged down to shatter on the tower's base. He would descend to his wife's prison then and, if he already had killed her, carry her wasted body to his own lands and bury it there. If he had left her alive, either because of some twisted moral scruple or out of a cruelty that passed beyond murder—then all he would have to do was to slip that gag into place again and wait for Murdock to resume his duties.

How long could my numbed hands keep their grasp? Two minutes? A little longer?

Feet pounding across the tower's tiled roof. The report of a pistol. Uncomprehending, not even curious, because it was almost as if I already had died, I rested my cheek against the stone and listened to the sounds of men locked in struggle—the shifting feet, the hoarse breathing, the impact of fist against flesh.

Another shot. A few seconds of silence. And then a voice I had thought never to hear again saying, "Don't look up. Don't even speak. Reach out with your left hand and draw the rope to you. Reach out, Elizabeth! There, that is right. Now grasp the rope with both hands. Hold on. Hold as fast as you can. I am going to draw you up."

I stared at the dark stones as he drew me past them. The rope was old and weakened by years of sun and rain and snow, and now it was bearing my full weight. If it broke, when I was only twenty inches or so from safety . . .

My upward motion stopped. From the tremors that ran along the rope, I knew he must be snubbing it around the crenelation from which the rope hung. Then I looked up and saw that he was leaning toward me over the parapet. His face, trying to mask its agonized tension with a smile, was only inches from my own.

For the first time in perhaps two hours, I thought, "The child." The unborn child that had made John turn from me in hatred and disgust. After tonight's ordeal, there might be no child.

"I am going to put my hands around your waist," John said. "When I do, grasp my upper arms as tightly as you can."

He drew me over the parapet and onto the tiles. I stood there in his arms, my trembling, exhausted body leaning against his. A few feet away, Clarence MacElvin lay sprawled, face upward to the starlight.

"Is he dead?"

"I don't know."

"Did you shoot him?"

"In a way. After he fired one pistol at me and missed, I

grappled with him. We were struggling for the second pistol when it went off. Can you stand alone while I drag
him inside onto the landing? Someone can attend to him
later. First I must get you back to the castle."

Twenty-six

I awoke to find my rooms filled with the brilliant light of sun reflected off snow. Almost immediately, as I lay there in the bed with its yellow hangings, I remembered with terrible clarity those hours in the tower. What was dream-like in my memory was my ride back across the snowy moor on the pommel of John's saddle. Dreamlike too was the memory of faces looking down at me after he had placed me on this bed,—the servants' faces, and Lady Macduveen's, for once shocked out of its placidity. Vaguely I remembered her asking what had happened to me. As nearly as I could recall, John had not answered her until after he had instructed the two maidservants to put me to bed, bandage my hands, and see to it that I drank some brandy. Then he had said, "We had best go outside, Lady Macduveen. I think you will want to send someone to the tower right away."

I heard a light tap on the door. One of the maids came in carrying a tray laden with a teapot and cup and saucer. I was still drinking the tea, lifting the cup in both my bandaged hands, when John knocked. He came in, drew a chair close to the bed, and sat down. "How do you feel?"

"Well enough." That was not true. My every muscle ached. But since I had not suffered what I feared most, a miscarriage, I preferred not to discuss my bodily state. Rather I wanted answers to my questions, especially one question. "John, why did you come back here last night?"

"You must know why. The coachman said that we had best go to Kyle Lochalsh, since the nearest inn was there. For over an hour, I sat in that coach hating you. Then I realized that the very intensity of my hatred proved how closely I was bound to you, and always would be bound. Perhaps I did not reason it out so clearly. All I know is that suddenly I was thinking, not of what you had told me, but of the look on your face when I called your child a bastard. I told the coachman to bring me back here as swiftly as he could."

The footman had led him to Lady Macduveen's sitting room. Donald and Mrs. MacElvin were with her. Both women seemed very upset.

"I know why now. Sometime earlier, as the MacElvins and Donald sat in the dining hall, the footman had come in to say that someone named Murray—"

"Murdock."

"Murdock was down in the courtyard with an urgent message. MacElvin had left, and not returned. But of course they did not tell me that when I first came back here last night. I asked to see you, and Lady Macduveen sent the footman to your room."

When the footman had returned to say that I was not there, John had asked for—or more likely demanded—the loan of a saddle horse, so that he might look for me. Old Angus, down in the stable, had told him the direction my

236

walks usually took.

"I saw the hoofprints of a galloping horse right away, and started to follow them. Then, off to the right, I saw your footprints."

My footprints had led him toward the grove of trees, and then, at an angle, toward the tower. "It was so damnably cold. Every time I saw a clump of gorse, I was afraid it was you huddled in the snow. When I was about a hundred yards from the tower, I heard you screaming."

For a moment we were both silent. Then I asked, "Is Clarence MacElvin—"

"He died just before daylight, several hours after Donald Macduveen and I brought him back here."

He had known he was dying, and so he had talked. Talked of the bribe he had taken secretly, of his fear that his wife would have him arrested for treason, and of his long imprisonment of her. At first her prison had been a sealed-off wing of his manor house, its only entrance a concealed one behind the wardrobe in his bedroom. Shortly before his bigamous marriage, he had taken her to the round tower.

John shuddered. "Do you know that even when he lay dying, he seemed to think that he would face God with one thing to his credit—his mercy in keeping his wife alive."

I had been afraid to ask about Arabella. I said with joyful relief, "Then she is alive!"

"Yes, she is here, in the room two doors from this one." He paused. "I questioned MacElvin about those attacks upon you. He admitted them. The first two, he said, had been designed only to frighten you away from here. If that pistol ball he fired into the courtyard had hit you, or if you had broken your neck on those stairs, I suppose he would have been able to tell himself that he was guiltless, since he had not intended to kill you. But by the time he forged that note, seeing you every time he came here had become such a torment to him that he actually did want you to drown in that bog."

No need to ask why my presence here had been a torment. To Clarence MacElvin it must have seemed that a malign fate had sent me to taunt him with the memory of the young, hate-filled and dangerous Arabella, and to keep him constantly reminded of that woman shut away in the tower. Perhaps he had even had a premonition that it would be through her grandniece that Arabella would be revenged.

I asked, "Will you be blamed for his death?"

"I doubt it. There will be an inquiry, of course. But your testimony and Arabella's, together with the confession all of us heard last night, should prevent any charge against me."

"Did his wife hear his confession?" John nodded. "Do you think she will testify?"

"If you had seen her face," he said dryly, "you would not need to ask that question. And it is she who is nursing that poor woman from the tower. I would judge, from the grim air of her, that she wants to atone for even having known Clarence MacElvin."

I asked, "And Murdock?"

"He is back in the tower with his falcons after spending the night in one of the sheds down in the courtyard. As soon as he talked to Clarence MacElvin last night, he must have collapsed."

"Will he be arrested?"

"Perhaps not, at his age, and with his addled wits. It all depends upon how such matters are handled in Scotland."

We were silent for a moment. Then he asked in a constrained voice, "Is the child—"

"I think the child is safe."

He took one of my bandaged hands gently in both of his. "Will you marry me, Elizabeth, and come home with me?"

Unable to speak, I nodded.

He bent and kissed my mouth. Then he straightened and said, "About the child."

My whole body became taut. Was he going to suggest that we arrange for some other couple to raise my child? I could not consent. I simply could not.

"Yes, John?"

"If it is a son, and if the name pleases you, I would like for us to name him William, after my father."

Twenty-seven

That morning is now fifteen years in the past. They have been good years, and not just because of John's steadfast love, or because of my tall son and my two little daughters. Our fellow townsmen, the people I remembered with such bitterness, have helped make them good years. I was still quite young when I returned from Scotland, and still fairly ignorant of human nature. I had not counted upon their contrition. But even though not once, in all these years, has anyone mentioned to me my father's banishment, they have all manifested their regret. They expressed it by visits they paid to us, first at the senior Harwoods' farm, and then at this house John built for us. After Will's birth, and those of the twins, they expressed it with an outpouring of jams and jellies and infant garments.

In my contentment, sometimes I pass whole months without thinking of Bowain Castle, and the tower, and Arabella. She is dead now, but she lived on for five years in the room that was first hers, and then mine, and then hers again. Did she ever walk again on the moors she had so loved, and find the lavender blossoms—"I have my own names for things"—which she called butterfly flowers? I do not know, because none of the long letters I have received from Aunt Dora, or the short, stiff ones from Lady Macduveen, have been much concerned with Arabella. But I hope she again felt heather springy under her feet, and heard a robin singing from a scarlet-berried rowan tree.

Because of my red-haired son, I am reminded more often of Charles Edward. Too, sometimes there are stories about him in the Boston paper that comes to us by packet boat. To me they are sad stories. A confirmed drunkard now, he has been deserted by Clementia Walkinshaw, who took their small daughter with her. He has not married. Perhaps he never will. It is possible that the little girl he has lost will be his only child—except, of course, for the tall boy who right now is chopping wood outside this kitchen window. And Charles Edward will never know about him.

He is a spirited boy, my son—as spirited as the man whose blood he carries unknowingly in his veins. Of late that quality has awakened in me apprehension as well as pride. Because there is revolutionary talk in our village and, I hear, in other colonies too. After town meeting now, in this summer of 1766, sober men gather outside the door and say the sort of things that my poor father, twenty years ago, was banished for saying in his cups at the tavern. No, the things they say are even more reckless. They do not advocate replacing King George—George the Third now—with some other monarch. The colonies, they say, should declare their independence of the crown!

It seems incredible to me that a few hundred thousand

241

farmers and blacksmiths and merchants would dare to re-
volt against the might of Britain. But neither John nor
Will finds the thought incredible.

Last night at supper Will turned to John, brown eyes
shining, and asked, "The war will not come too soon, will
it, Father? Not while I am still too young to fight?"

"I think not, Son. These matters take time." John added
wryly, "It may not come until I am too old to fight."

I thought, looking at his beloved face, "I hope it does
not come until then!"

My gaze turned to my son. The phrase, "The last of the
Stuarts," came into my head. I thought of the wild and
beautiful land of his ancestors, and of my wet cloak spread
to dry before a fire in Bowain Wood. I thought of Charles
Edward beside me in that room in the Russell Square
house, and of the icy stiffness of the rope in my hands as
John drew me and my unborn child up to safety. And I
felt awed by the beauty and terror of life, and by its cruel-
ties and its mercies.

And by the strange turnings it can take. Perhaps there is
one more such turning ahead. Perhaps a few years from
now my son will march with other Southampton men
down the tree-lined village street, and I, with fear and
pride in my heart, will watch him go. Red-haired Will
Harwood of Southampton, going off to fight—and pray
God to win!—against the successor of that King George
red-haired Charles Edward fought against—and lost.